FLIP TURN

FLIP TURN

PAULA EISENSTEIN

Mansfield Press

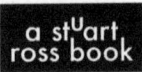

Copyright © Paula Eisenstein 2012
All Rights Reserved
Printed in Canada

Library and Archives Canada Cataloguing in Publication

Eisenstein, Paula
    Flip turn / Paula Eisenstein.

Issued also in electronic formats.
ISBN 978-1-894469-82-1

    I. Title.

PS8609.I745F55 2012   C813'.6   C2012-906015-1

Editor for the Press: Stuart Ross
Design: Denis De Klerck
Typesetting: Stuart Ross
Cover Image: Shutterstock
Author Photo: Larry Eisenstein

The publication of *Flip Turn* has been generously supported by the Canada Council for the Arts and the Ontario Arts Council.

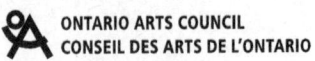

Mansfield Press Inc.
25 Mansfield Avenue, Toronto, Ontario, Canada M6J 2A9
Publisher: Denis De Klerck
www.mansfieldpress.net

Inside you now's another,
thrashing like a fish,
swinging, fighting,
for its inch already.

— Michael Ondaatje, "A House Divided"

1

PECKING ORDER

In our family there's an order. First is my mother, then my father, then, by age, my brother, me, my sister. When we're driving to Gaspé in the summer to visit my mother's parents, my sister is always in the middle on the lump.

I would never give up my window seat and neither would my brother. The middle is for squirmers and sweaters. We look at each other overtop of our sister's head with distant eyes, regal and prevailing, our pupils small from looking at the vistas out the windows on our opposite sides of the car.

My mother sits in the front passenger seat, her left arm draped across the seatbacks. I sit behind her so she can't get such a good swing at me when she's in a swatting mood.

Cal, my brother, behind my dad, is in prime position for the side of her hand.

Sometimes the order can get switched and I get a promotion ahead of my brother because of being a girl, because of being the same as my mother. But getting too much of an advantage over him would mean him hating me more so the best is to try to stick with my regular position.

THEORETICAL

It's worse to be the first child because even if you get the most attention it's still the worst position to be in when the next kid comes along. It's the most shocking. At least when my little sister Cindy came along I was used to there being too many kids and not enough attention.

Still my sister was really disgusting. She was mewly. You know how when kittens are taken away from their mother too young, they make little mewing sounds. We call it making pancakes, what they do with their paws, little paw-alternating pressing motions, which is actually the motion to make the mother cat's milk come down. That was my sister. Completely needy.

RED HAIR

My mom has red hair. Bright red hair. Flaming. Hysterical. And freckles. A lot of freckles all over the place. But she also tans well. A lot of red-haired people don't tan well. She has droopy green eyes with yellow middles and the most meagre pale eyelashes.

I wish I had Shannon Williams' mom whose voice always sounds sweet, soft and reasonable and whose colouring is much more relaxing.

If we're bad, mom puts us with our noses in the corner. We stand and wait until she says. Other times she comes after us swinging and screeching with an orangey-pink flyswatter and you're wondering if it has some leftover yellow bug juice on it.

The time she was really happy was when she got a long cord for the phone so she could do all the things in the kitchen while she was talking. But her phone is green, olive green, not black like the boring neighbours' phones. It's warm and pretty, the same as her eyes.

THE ARGUMENT

One time mom and dad were arguing so badly with each other that my dad slammed the door and left the house.

I was lying on the floor on my stomach colouring the same boring colour until I noticed the empty feeling. Like all along we were in a swimming pool only I didn't realize it until suddenly the pool was full so I had no choice but to start swimming. So I decided to cry. That's what was different. It wasn't like a regular cry because it was a decision. But it was still real. Like a mother at a funeral might need to take a moaning run at it, knowing the grief will surface, it just needs to be tapped into.

So my mom was the argument winner.

CAL'S IDEA

Since dad was smoking but hiding it from us but we knew, Cal had an idea for a trick to catch him out. Because Cal was in trouble all the time and smoking behind our parents' back only they knew, his idea was to put an empty cigarette package on the floor of the coat room, but when he was caught and accused he would claim innocence because it wasn't his brand, it was dad's, so dad would have to confess.

It was nice Cal talking to us, me and Cindy. Cal didn't talk to us much anymore. It wasn't hard to help him with his plan. We didn't need to do anything. His telling us was our job so we could be his witnesses.

Some things Cal had done wrong lately were he had a girl over to the house one time and was criticizing the way mom decorates. Actually that's an example of something I say he did wrong—our parents didn't know about that. What was so wrong about it was it's the thing mom can't be criticized for. Our house is the only one that's colourful and with antiques from trips to Gaspé.

Next Cal streaked, which is where you run naked, around the neighbourhood with underwear on his head. Also, he tried to buy some pot but it wasn't pot. He was sad and so was my mom because it was his old best friend who betrayed him by selling him the fake pot. There was a darkness in his friend for doing that, but it was like a trick of the light because you could feel it. You could feel how his friend wasn't in trouble but Cal was. Then he painted his room chocolate brown and put a red exit light for the light in the ceiling, had a black beanbag chair and was listening to music and smoking in his room the whole time.

WAFTING

Where we ended up was in the middle of the afternoon, me in my bedroom in the basement, Cindy in her bedroom where Cal's used to be but back to being painted normal, dad on his recliner with his arm down the side with the smoke wafting up, pretending not to be smoking but not so much as before.

What I have a lot of on my bedroom walls are big posters of cats I taped up. Pumas, cougars. I like them because they're beautiful and ferocious. Their fur looks so soft, you want to touch it, pet them. But how are you going to get past the wildness to getting your want?

The saddest sadness is your dad's because he's always never showing it. He's always better than it. He's your dad with his jumpy step, taking care of it, even though how he does it comes with a scowl and disappointment in what you should have done.

Could we please go back to school? There weren't ever any sirens wailing for that day but I always hear them anyway.

Back in my Friday afternoon grade eight classroom, my teacher, Mr. Whalen, says, "What was it about? Was it about you and me?"

ADVANTAGES

Mr. Whalen is tall and skinny with big goggle eyes you can see even through his glasses, a wispy moustache and loose but tidy suits.

A great thing about Mr. Whalen is that he never gives me less than an A on writing assignments. Mr. Whalen loves my writing.

Poor Julie Pollard, my best friend who is really smart, so smart that she was supposed to accelerate from grade three to five, but couldn't because her very mean older sister was in that class, so it wasn't possible, wanted Mr. Whalen for her grade eight teacher, but didn't get him. She got Mr. McCrae, the science teacher with the sideways greasy bang hair and the sweating.

Another example of Julie's intelligence is she could make rhyming poems as good as Dr. Seuss already only in grade three. I remember it. Her wan eyes begging under too long bangs.

Julie's being the fifth child of her family and after her are two more adopted native Indian brothers explains why she is especially good at figuring out who is going to like her and why she was so bummed out about not getting Mr. Whalen.

GOING ON

But why would Mr. Whalen say to me right then, so stupidly and meanly, "Was it about you and me?" I keep my boisterousness under control.

Not that it really was so mean, just insensitive, but only especially insensitive because of the timing of the day. What was the problem he was thinking of between us that could mean my going away and discussing it so long?

What could be so bad about me that I didn't already know?

CLASS

Because I like Mr. Whalen's class. Julie's right. It is better. It has the square green-on-the-sides desks with the chairs you pull in and out. Mr. McCrae's class has the all-in-one desks, which are clunky-looking and different-sized making his room look sloppy. Also his room faces east so the blackboards always have glare on them in the morning but ours faces west so it's always cool-feeling and relaxed.

Our class feels quiet in an effective, superior way. And in the afternoons we move around, called going on rotation, to other classes with other teachers so it doesn't matter that the sun comes pouring in too hard in the afternoon.

I was second top student in my grade seven class last year after Jill Davies.

ARRIVING

Mr. Farrell, the principal, gets me from class and walks me down to the office. My sister is there already and my dad too. The office is bleached, bland whitey yellow with grey parts like the typewriter and its typewriter ticking sound. Stale cigarette smell and haze from the teachers' lounge. Mr. Farrell lifts his arm from beside his leg partway up, gesturing us into his office, just us for privacy.

It's nice of him to give us his office, a chubby bumbling man with shaggy hair and an oversized moustache combining to make him look inefficient. Maybe now that he's given it up he's feeling awkward, foiled once again by his own generosity, stuck on the wrong side of his office door with nothing to do, useless alongside his capable, competent typing secretary.

Dad's hesitating. The sirens still aren't wailing, just the empty sound. It's not our mom. Our mom is okay. When I find out she's okay all the other stuff coming tumbling down and adding up and putting all the evidence of the past week together like a logical conclusion isn't so bad.

THE WINTER BEFORE

Luckily Cal got out of trouble because of being under age from what he did the winter before, which was take a car he stole and drive it around a slippery bend and crash it.

AIR RAID SIREN

There is an actual siren. It's the same height as the row of pine trees in the backyard of the school that are still there from when it was a farmer's field. It's painted grey to match the sky on a hazy summer day if you were ever there, if your mom were to allow you to try one of the school summer camps.

It's closest to the kindergarten door for recess and the basketball hoops. It must have just got put up one day.

LYING

When mom learned about the girl who was found dead at the Y and they were looking for a suspect about possible foul play, she phoned Cal right away—he was living at the Hardy Geddes Home for Troubled Teenagers downtown on Queen Street—and demanded to know if he had anything to do with it.

Mom has that way about her of grilling you so fiercely you know you're going to tell the truth. That's why the best defense against her is if you lie really good to yourself, so that you convince even yourself. After mom got off the phone with Cal there was the feeling of accomplishment, hands dusting themselves off, no problem and everything taken care of.

SO THAT'S WHAT IT WAS

Being a kid in a family sometimes your job is being protected and staying innocent. It becomes your responsibility. Trusting what you're told for your own good. Getting decided upon.

There was some information in the newspaper. That dad was the father. I couldn't understand why they would bring up who was the father, because dad didn't do it.

WHAT I SAID

What I said to Mr. Whalen when he asked was it about him and me, was, "No, it's not that." Then something like, "You'll find out." Partly because I could see he was worried about this thing about us he was thinking about and needed reassurance and partly because I didn't want to have to tell him. I wasn't ready for it to start yet.

WHAT JULIE SAID

After school my best friend Julie and I practiced taking shots on the basketball hoops outside the kindergarten doors. It was practically like a warm summer day only it was November. Julie said, "What are you going to do?"

2

FRIDAY NIGHTS

I'm an excellent swimmer. Seriously excellent. I've already been city champion three times. Now I'm a provincial champion with a provincial record.

Friday nights, which is tonight, swim practice is at Beal Tech. Whoever built Beal's pool wasn't thinking about helping swimmers swim fast. It's old-style, with big gutters and tall walls. The water is extremely choppy. I don't know what they were thinking. Beal's water is pushing you around and your mind isn't on swimming fast either, it's on where are the ladders in case I need to make a quick exit.

Beal is also where the high schoolers have their swim championships. London high school swim records must be very slow. But we're only at Beal one night a week. The rest of the time practice is at the downtown Y in the mornings and in the evenings at the Bob Hayward Y.

BATHING SUIT

One time we were at a swim meet up at the university and Cal's bathing suit was falling down, it was practically down around his knees, his bare bum wiggling just a few inches below the water. It was a green bathing suit because it was a swim meet and we wear our team colours at swim meets. But he wouldn't stop to fix it. He just kept on swimming. He wasn't even going very fast. He wasn't even having a good race.

Cal has a bit of a herky-jerky motion when he swims. Every time he turns his head to breathe, there's this little lull where his forward progress halts. It's not very magnificent. I don't know why he does that.

PSYCHOPATH

The reason why Cal is getting off for murder is because it turns out he's a psychopath with no feelings. A lot of people think this is a trick to do with the lawyer my mom and dad got for him. Only they don't say it to my face.

If Cal had feelings he would know to feel bad for killing the girl, only he didn't really kill her, it was an accident, but he did have it in his mind to hurt her if he didn't get what he wanted, so that's a psychopath, because he didn't care afterwards.

What he wanted was to have sex with her whether she wanted to or not. He wanted to rape her. But then when he couldn't he pushed her down the stairs.

MEAN

Sometimes there's still a few high school kids hanging around the hallways at Beal but if there are, they just keep where they are. They don't bother us. It's different from what I'm used to because whenever high school kids come by my school they act mean.

Even though the outside of the school looks so old, the hallways have modern lights and tiles and lockers. Mostly the locker doors are all closed but sometimes one is hanging open and when you close it, it makes a cold slamming sound echo down the empty halls. There's a slightly gluey smell and always some fluffy piles of dust mixed with hair along the walls.

We line up along the floor, leaning on the walls, waiting for a coach to arrive and open the locker room and the pool.

DOLLY

Dolly sits demurely with the rest of us like if she blends in soft enough it will change the fact she doesn't belong. Her body is soft and already full-bosomed. She has strawberry blond hair, frizzy and to her shoulders. She says nothing.

I think the reason she's here is because her parents own the variety store right across the street from the Bob Hayward

Y and the idea of Dolly being on the swim team was too handy for them to ignore. Something serious must have happened to Dolly because she has a glass eye.

I've never paid attention to where they put her when we're swimming. She must be in the slow lane but she's too slow. When is she going to figure out she's too slow for the slow lane? She's too old to be able to improve enough to swim with us. She's too soft. She is never going to be good enough.

WHAT'S GOOD ABOUT BEAL

A lot of times at Beal on Friday nights we get to do fun things, not just swim lengths for two hours straight. We get to practice relay races, do stroke drills and work on improving our flip turns, which are the somersault turns you do at the end of the pool for changing directions. Also there are substitute coaches more often on Friday nights, willing to have fun and not so concerned about what they need to make us do to perform better at swim meets.

When we first started at Beal our coach was Gus Paxton. Now it's Sally Healy.

THE COACH WE HAD BEFORE

Gus Paxton is handsome with a muscular swimmer's chest, slightly long blond hair, not afraid of wearing only his bathing suit so his chest shows, even though he's swim coach and on the deck, not in the water.

Cal and I are walking onto the deck of the big pool at the Y for practice at the same time. It doesn't usually work out we enter quite so precisely together. We go through separate boys' and girls' locker rooms. We do different things to prepare that take different amounts of time.

Seeing us coming in together gives Gus the idea for a good pun on our last name in front of a bunch of the older kids surrounding him being smart and laughing, so now they're laughing even more. At us. Gus continues on how we are such slackers. Slackers are lazy and don't work hard during swim practice.

For me I know it's true. One time I got out and went and sat in the bathroom in the middle of practice when I didn't even have to go. Just for a break. Because it's hard. A lot of times what I want is to stop and not swim round in circles anymore.

The advantage of the sport of swimming is that when you're in the water doing lengths you could cry like a baby if you wanted to without people knowing. Everything's already wet so the tear marks don't show. If someone were to ask, "Why is your face so red?" you would just say, "It's from the exertion."

RED FACE

I completely don't get Ellen Musgrave. Her hair is red but not as much as my mom's. She already has very nice breasts in her bathing suit but not bulging. They look like the way a regular woman's breasts look advertising white button-up blouses with only the top button or two undone in the Sears catalogue even though for swim meets she's only in the eleven to twelve age group. She's towards the top of the age group.

Ellen stays to the other side of the deck keeping away from Gus Paxton but she's also glaring at him with her face getting red from the anger. She looks like the cartoon characters with steam coming out of their ears, but she's not trying to be funny.

Why is she making herself so obvious? If I was able to be myself as far as she is being herself, wouldn't I be able to tell on him too? But the way I am, which is walking around him too, is always like it didn't happen. I'm walking around him like if I'm good and pretend hard enough everything is normal, he won't do it again because my acting job will convince him so well that even he will think it didn't happen.

We were in the little pool at the Y because he picked me for flip turn practice. Getting chosen for flip turn practice, which is to help you improve your form and speed for turning at the end of the length of the pool, is the greatest reprieve. It means all the other kids are still doing lengths but you're getting a break.

But how Gus does it is he holds you in a flat floating position facing the wall ready to launch to practice your turn. Then he wriggles and sneaks his fingers under your bathing suit and digs them right in your crotch, so his fingers are actually sticking inside of you. It burns. Then he pushes you towards the wall, releases, and you do your flip. He keeps doing that, each time the surprise of it, until practice is over and you walk to your locker and sit in front of it on the bench that's there.

And hope he never picks you again.

LEARNING TO SWIM

I don't remember learning to swim. Actually a lot of people don't. I took a survey. It's because swimming is very primordial. Primordial, like back when Earth was a creepy stew of dinosaurs and scaly things peering at you out of lagoons.

I don't know how I got to be such a great swimmer either. It's like it just happened. Maybe it's the exposure. My brother and sister are good swimmers too, just not as good as me. Every summer our family would either rent a cottage in Bayfield, which is nearby on Lake Huron, visit our across the street neighbour Eunice's cottage also nearby in Sparta on Lake Erie or drive down to the ocean in Gaspé, in Quebec.

Only we say it Gasbee, proudly like we know better, which we do, because it's where my mom was born and that's how she says it, not in an ignorant way, like she's not aware that everyone else pronounces it Gaspay, the way you're supposed to, because it's a French word and has a French accent, but because her family, which is Scottish, has lived there for over a hundred and fifty years, and that's just how you say it when you're from there.

DOUBLE BED

The summer before I found out about being an excellent swimmer was a Bayfield year. A lot of times in Bayfield we rent from the Wileys but sometimes from the Johnsons too. The problem with the Johnsons is the sleeping arrangement situation, the having to share a double bed with my sister who is almost a year and a half younger than me. To deal with it, mostly I'm just mad at her all the time. My idea with my sister is: here's a line right down the middle of the room, now you stay on your side.

It's hard to sleep mad and on your own side all night especially in the Johnsons' bed, which is soft and saggy and forces you to the middle whether you want to or not. Since I'm trying so hard not to touch her it's hard to sleep. Then I lie in bed awake after she falls asleep, knowing the still of the dark and the amount of light coming through the blinds from the streetlights and the moon and the quietness.

TUNES

My mom is friends with Joan Wiley who stays at her own cottage when we're not renting it from her, when we're renting from the Johnsons. Her body is slim at the top but with big legs at the bottom. She wears grey skirts to her knees that show her big legs from where she sits on the soft chairs in her cottage smiling. I can tell how much my mom loves talking to her by the way she doesn't get excited when it turns out my brother Cal can pick out tunes on the piano by ear.

SEA MOON

For Bayfield's annual parade mom makes Cal into a pirate and me and Cindy into hippies mostly out of beach towels. After the parade we paint pictures, on a wall made special for the occasion out of white painted plywood, for prizes. Cal's painting is called an abstract painting. He paints wiggly lines in bright green and yellow and black. He paints peace signs and spells out the word peace. He gets his picture in the newspaper.

Mine has a black background that takes a long time to fill in with a yellow moon in the top corner. In the middle is the space rocket Apollo 11 flying to the moon. I don't care that Cal gets a picture of himself and his painting in the newspaper. I love my painting and just because his picture is in the newspaper doesn't mean it's better than mine.

My brother's suntanned body is fat in the tummy. Sometimes when he's concentrating he puts the paintbrush in his mouth and his hand on his hip so his stomach's sticking out even more.

When Apollo 11 gets to the moon in two days it's going to land in a sea. It's going to land in the Sea of Tranquility.

BLOCK PARENTS

What I don't get is how Cal can be the one that is the psychopath. He's so stupid. A psychopath is supposed to be smart, manipulating everyone to get exactly what he wants. But Cal would always be getting in trouble.

One time some big kids from his grade were after him probably because he wouldn't shut his mouth about something and he actually went to a Block Parent's house. Block Parents are the ones that put the red and white sign in their window of a kid holding up his arm to an adult, meaning if you're in trouble and need help you can go there. Only nobody ever does it, goes to a Block Parent, except Cal did.

The poor Block Parent called my mom to do something. She said there were some big kids out in front of her house who wanted to beat him up. She needed my mom's help and didn't know what to do.

What I know for getting along: whatever Cal does, just do the opposite. That's all there is to it.

HOME

After swim practice Friday night mom is there. She talks to me and Cindy. What we are to do is, "Don't milk it." That means we're not supposed to use the situation of what Cal did to get special advantages from her or other people. That's the conversation and what she thinks we're thinking about.

3

MONDAY

Going back to school Monday morning is tricky because we have a dentist appointment. We can't skip the dentist appointment because that wouldn't be normal. But coming into school late Monday morning is like putting a big neon sign over your head flashing, "Brother charged with murder! Brother charged with murder!" Aren't we supposed to not be drawing attention to the situation and ourselves?

Plus when I enter the classroom it's like everyone is staring at me and everyone knows. And I'm trying to say, "No, it's not that, everything's cool, everything's under control, it was just a dentist appointment." Only what's the point of saying that? Nobody's going to believe me even though it is true. We were at the dentist.

And I can feel Mr. Whalen's eyes and I can feel my old best friend Shannon from three doors down and one across who's not best friends with me anymore because, well, she's just way more cool than me and wears platform shoes and blue eye shadow, and I can tell by how she's looking at me that she knows and her family knows. I can feel all of their sadness for me, only if I let myself go in that direction, the direction of feeling it would be like going out of control to where my mom said is not allowed. What I know is right and safe is what she said—to not "milk it."

Also it's my second period. And there's a big wad of awkward paper product between my legs that won't get in a good position under my jeans. It feels like a diaper. It feels like I'm going back to being a baby again and I don't want to.

JEWISH FRIENDS

Mom really liked me for my first period.

We were in the basement in the laundry room that was recently renovated into a bathroom too, behind one of those folding doors, when I told her. The floor used to be cement but now there's linoleum tiles over it so it looks nicer. But there's still the drain hole there.

She was all loud and screechy like she is but this time happy, not yelling mad. Mom's been making new friends since she opened her own bookstore downtown. Her having a lot of

Jewish friends she talks to on the sofas in the back room of the store means there's other cultures in the world besides regular white people. There's actually been a Chinese girl in our class called Sandra Chan for a long time. There's a German girl too.

Did I know that the Jewish tradition when the daughter starts her period is to slap her? I think she's going to tell them about it happening to me and that it will be okay. I wonder if she's going to tell my dad though. The thought of her telling him makes me feel like he might not like it, that when he finds out he's going to be disappointed in me.

WHO I LIKE

I never go to the Friday night dances. I have swim practice anyway so I wouldn't be allowed. One time I joined the basketball team and got home too late for swim practice. It was a really bad game because that same week in practice my best friend Julie Pollard forgot what direction our team was going in and shot at our own team's basket.

You simply can't forget that kind of thing. How I acted for her shooting at the wrong basket was to hold myself off very aloof and talk in a cool, formal voice. But then, in this actual game, I did the same thing. In a real game. Then it was too late for my dad to take me to swim practice and the message that came through the phone from my mom was, "We can't be spending money on your training to become a great swimmer and then you're missing all these practices for basketball games."

It's not crass. I'm not saying that. I mean there's no way I could possibly quit swimming. Swimming is what I do.

Besides, if I'm Ontario Champion, doesn't that prove that we're all okay, that our family is fine? There's nothing wrong with us.

But what if Jack Hayes were to ask me to the dance?

JACK HAYES

Since kindergarten I've been tied for tallest kid in the class with Rose Panner. Next after us is Brad Mullins. I thought I might be doomed to be boyfriend–girlfriend with Brad Mullins because besides being tall he's loud, which so am I. In kindergarten I was the main kid in the class who couldn't remember to put their hand up for asking questions the way you're supposed to. Brad was the other. Also his hair is quite curly like mine. I thought getting out of being with him would be like fighting against gravity. Like trying stopping being the word chosen to rhyme in a poem.

When I was in grade six and got a blue with white polka dots hot-pants suit for my birthday, but because it was winter with leotards on underneath, Brad's idea was to give me such hard birthday spankings I could feel them a long time after recess was over in my backbone like some of the winter cold had got in there too.

Jack Hayes isn't as big as Brad, but okay-sized and not too skinny. I don't want to be with a guy I feel like I'm going to knock over. But mostly I can tell guys like that don't want to be with me. Like if there's a circle of kids and they're in it, they're going to put their elbows out and try not to let you in.

Like Terry Aitkin could. Terry's desk is right beside mine but angled a bit in front, sometimes more, depending on how the janitor swept the floor and put the desks for the week. Terry cracks jokes all class. Not in a noisy way so he disrupts things and has to get everyone's attention, just quiet so only I can hear, or Jack who sits in front of him, or Janice behind me.

It's the same with how he gets to school. Since Terry lives behind the school on the other side of the school fence, instead of walking all the way around the fronts of the houses to the front school entrance, he and his brother just throw their bags over, then climb the tall chain-link fence with the sharp stick-out bits that can rip your clothes at the top but avoid doing that and jump down. That's it. The teachers on yard duty always say, "Don't do that," to them, but they still do it. Like with the jokes, it's not to draw attention or be a problem. Because why should they waste all that time walking all the way around when they can just jump over?

And Terry Aitkin doesn't act like my bigness is a problem for him. He doesn't make his eyes go cold and push at you with them to a spot a little farther away, not smile at you with them because that might draw you in and make the problem of your being bigger closer. But when I look at Terry hard he's got this nervous quivering quality that could be exactly that, or maybe more like all of life is trying to squeeze him down and he's a flea with a hard shell that gives him withstanding powers. But that's the problem again because someone as big as me wouldn't suit a flea.

The joke we do with each other is feigning passionate admiration for each other's knees. Terry has those brown eyes that aren't too brown along with the kind of dark eyelashes that clump together in separate sections making the eyelashes look really big. He has the big dark and obvious kind of freckles on his face further accenting his eyes because of the freckle colour matching the eye colour. He has a short chin and a wide mouth giving him a crazy long grin. Once, for a writing assignment I wrote an ode to his knees. I got an A.

I'm usually like the boss of my section of the class since I get high marks and am paying attention. But with Terry I let him be boss too, even if he doesn't care about high marks. I let him because how he is and how he sees things is so good but he lets me keep being boss in my way too.

FUNNY TOO

Janice who sits behind me can be really funny too but not so often. She has pale skin like a porcelain doll but tries hard not to be pretty with short hair and wears unfashionable slim-legged boys' pants when bell-bottoms or flares is the style, even in the summer. It's her first year at our school and she doesn't even try to make friends.

Her eyes are sad but not like those big droopy, feel-sorry-for-yourself sad eyes, just soft and bleak like it's not worth trying. Only her chin juts out, very determined-like, at the same time.

KITCHEN RENO

When Cal started getting funny was around the same time mom renovated the kitchen. She took down the cupboards that divided the dining from the kitchen area turning it into a big kitchen-dining space in the style of an old farm kitchen.

Cal didn't tell jokes that he learned from a joke book. He just figured out a way of making things funny in the moment. Mom is like that too, so they were going back and forth with each other in the new kitchen with the new sliding glass doors letting in extra light and the cupboards newly painted a sophisticated antique blue.

Then I wanted to learn how to be funny too.

GRAB

Another time Cal showed Aunt Sylvia how to drive me to ballet class and she was complimenting him and that's when I realized you could look out and know where you're going and not depend on grown-ups, that he knew about directions, that there were directions. Then we were at our neighbour Eunice's cottage playing checkers and he beat me every time without even trying. I was so mad that mom told me to go outside of the cottage because of Eunice's headache. Then I was too close to the cliff where some of the polluters dump their garbage, you can see it where the cliff meets the road over on the other side, which Eunice and mom are very against. I was falling only I grabbed a branch and screamed, the fear of almost falling down a cliff, although there was a bit of a slope to it, my heart beating in my temples.

Mom only saying, "Be quiet," and "Can't you pay attention to that Eunice has a headache?"

MORE HATEFUL

The reason why I'm worse than Cal is because I know what it's like to want to beat your older brother, to be better, but because of his being the oldest he never had to feel that. How could he be the manipulator when he doesn't even know, when he is so stupid?

Take Christmas. Cal made mom and dad miserable always wanting more. When all you have to do is watch what he does and act the opposite, make everybody happy. Don't want more. Then everyone will love you.

SWIM TIP # 1—PASSING ETIQUETTE

If you're swimming along, everything's fine but your nose keeps getting right in the person's feet in front of you, it means you need to pass them. The worst thing to do is just grab on to their ankle, yank them under and swim on top of them because I've had it happen before. Show some consideration. You almost go immobile and drown when it happens to you, trying to understand why anyone would do that.

The best is to tap on their foot or ankle or thigh, wherever it is you've swum up to on their body. And then their job is to pull aside a bit, then stop at the end of the length to let you pass.

You should tap a few times. It's a delicate situation because too many times might be considered annoying. But people don't always notice the first tap.

If they ignore you, it's tempting to do what's called cutting off, which is when you stop about five metres before the end of the pool length, turn back in the direction you came from, and just go in front of them. I'm not saying don't do it, just don't do it too much because it's very close to cheating, which if you do too much is a whole other problem.

When I say tap, I don't mean like a tap where you're stopped and standing and knocking gently at someone's front door. You're swimming. Obviously you can't stop to pass. What you have to do is touch their body while you're in your swimming motion. That's what I mean by tap. It's difficult. Try not to let your fingernails claw them.

Overall, be careful not to get kicked in the face.

HIDING

Some of us grade eights are in the upstairs hallway when we should have been outside already for recess five minutes ago. Then a teacher is coming up the side stairwell. "Run and hide," I whisper-yell, so we run for it clomping like camels to the art room and hide under the art room desks. It's easy for Mr. Whalen to find us because of the giggling and before that the noisy running.

But Mr. Whalen is specifically mad at me in a quiet voice in front of the other kids because of, I've changed. That's what he says: "You've changed."

4

MORNING ROUTINE

Dad comes to get me a little after five to take me to morning swim practice. Usually I'm already awake by the time he opens the door and he doesn't get to the gentle shoulder shake part. My secret psychic power: sensing when my dad's going to wake me up.

Everything looks jangly in the morning, quiet, like the atoms in objects are spread out too much and you can see right into the spaces between them. Dad and I are like ghosts moving too quick or too slow for the time, mom still asleep. I loathe toast with thick slabs of honey on it. I hate weird shakes with that bitty part of the egg that the blender can't blend floating somewhere in it and going to find my tongue eventually.

What makes dad crazy in the pre-dawn night is the traffic light on the way to the Y at the end of Kipps Lane. Sometimes our neighbour Bruce Ferguson is getting a ride to swim practice too. Or we're picking up Stan Milton along the way. Turning left on Adelaide, because during regular driving hours Kipps Lane is such a small side street compared to Adelaide, the light takes a very long time to change. It's intolerable, his hand beating on the steering wheel, his head looking up and down Adelaide Street at no traffic, nothing, his neck craning around looking back at how there's no one to see him do it, if he were to go ahead and do it, make a break for it, run the light and be damned. He's scowling.

Dad's transporting me in my blissful warm cocoon of wishing for just this once that practice could be cancelled from storm winds that rage too violently, of power outages affecting indispensable pool mechanisms, from coach forgetting to change his clock when the time changes. I envision benign catastrophes while savouring the last minutes before the inevitable cold crush of water bangs against my skin pressing past my sleepy comfort, pushing me hard into my morning ritual. Under water only exertion from the bones will help me find a warmth again.

Eventually the light changes. I am imagining other possible reprieves on the road ahead.

MAYBE ANGELA WHITE

Behind the tall front desk at the downtown YMCA, Francine Passero, assistant manager of customer services, wants to see me. Behind the big curly eyelashes and soft pink skin, she wants to see me because of the graffiti in the dryer room.

The dryer room is the dark area behind the ladies' membership plus that connects the girls' and the women's locker rooms. The dryers are big metal octopus arms like from Jules Verne's *Twenty Thousand Leagues Under the Sea* that emanate from the high ceiling. You twist them how you like and aim them at your hair. Because it's so curly I can blow dry my hair into an Afro. It's the style.

Francine wants to know if it was me who put up the huge red lettering in huger red hearts about me and Hanley Bell.

It's like she thinks I don't know my brother killed someone in this very same building. That I don't know that his name, the same last name as mine, the same last name in the hearts with Hanley Bell, isn't a good name to be writing up in the dryer room lately. Like she doesn't know it's hard and I'm trying my best to be in the same building with it every day. Can't they see that?

I really don't know who would do it. I can only think of someone who is my competition. Angela White used to be my biggest competition.

CRANE OPERATOR

She was doing better than I was and my mom was in the balcony watching me training, the same balcony the papers said was where Selena was last seen before she was killed. My mom said, "Why aren't you working as hard as Angela?"

This was before though. Before Angela's big swimmer's shoulders got too sore and started going soft because the ice wasn't enough. Before when her parents used to come and watch her too, her dad, with his big dumb round crane-operator face, the curly hair receding to a little bun at the top of his head, her mom colder, bad white skin and behind glasses. Then she wasn't doing so well in school anymore either. She was hanging out in the back with the smokers and the dopers.

Nobody ever sees Angela anymore with her pointy-toe walk, her pale skin that she started getting small tattoos burnt on, her skinny paler little brother in tow with his quiet mangled air from being Gus Paxton's favourite. Her chlorine-bleached greenish hair going back to being normal.

OUT TO GET ME

Even Yvonne Nowak is taking potshots. We're changing in the locker room after practice and she's telling me how she's glad she has the straight kind of shoulders, how the straight ones are the better kind.

I'm asking her questions to get to the bottom of the implications. Because Yvonne's parents are even poorer than Angela's. Because she can only get to morning practice every day out of the goodness of Jim McNeal's, Tommy McNeal's father's, heart. Because her parents don't even have a car and her father's old and coughing and wears undershirts looking out the window and can't speak English. Because if you've ever waited in the hallway of her place, the top floor of a house with a small porch on a main street with caked-on dirt that no one washes off, it has that really bad smell of someone always cooking turnips or maybe cabbage getting into everything, cooking all day long.

Everybody knows even though no one knows about the McNeals' helpfulness because Tommy McNeal and his dad Jim McNeal and the other McNeals have a lot of reasons to forget to be discreet and mention it a lot. Yvonne who has straight-across shoulders is telling me whose shoulders are more curvy-down how the straight ones are the better ones. Yvonne Nowak!

What I do is pretend that mine are the same kind, like I'm too generous and obtuse to get what she's getting at, like her definition encompasses all shoulder types. Yvonne is smart enough to argue me some more if she wants to.

When Yvonne came to Canada she was five and was playing in the schoolyard with only cement and no grass, not knowing how to speak English. Now she has tidy, compliant handwriting. She hasn't connected her prettiness to any purpose, so it's like she isn't. She's getting used to the problem of being the girl who's helped. So she'll just have to settle for only being better than me in her head because she can tell I'm not budging.

THE IDEA OF THE TWO-BEAT KICK

It's all the rage, from Australia, the two-beat kick, the purpose of which is to conserve energy for distance swimmers. A regular kick for freestyle is four or six beats or kicks per stroke. It's Sally Healy's, my best ever coach except for this, idea to convert me to it.

Why it turns out to not be smart is I'm not a long-distance swimmer. My first ever Ontario championship win, in which I set a new provincial record, was the one hundred metre freestyle, a sprint! Though I'm more a middle-distance swimmer than a sprinter really.

Converting to a two-beat kick is hard because you have to break the habit of your natural way. But the converting back is even worse, especially because it's Sally Healy doing it, urging you on, frustrated, acting like it isn't all her fault you're having the problem of switching back in the first place. You get used to the ease of expending less energy with the two-beat kick.

When my mom, who made friends with Sally so got some training tips from her, goes to the Y for a swim to get exercise she still does the two-beat kick. She still thinks it's the greatest. She could swim like that forever.

CANDY

Mom always makes friends with the regular Y lifeguards too. That's why Brita, one of the lifeguards and also an instructor, knows how the t-shirt I'm wearing is my first swimming t-shirt from my first swim meet outside of London. It's white, almost to my knees, with a square blue outline of a box on the chest with the words inside the box, also in blue, saying "Etobicoke Swim Club" on it. Every time Brita sees me at the Saturday Morning Fun Club she notices I'm wearing it and is smiling and saying something to me about it.

Cal doesn't do Saturday Morning Fun Club. He's too old. He does judo. Saturday Morning Fun Club and judo are bonus activities we do at the Y besides swim club, the reason why we joined.

For Saturday Morning Fun Club you go to different activities all through the building all morning and the early part of the afternoon with other kids the same age. You're a colour. You read on the chart under your colour what activity you're going to next. Saturday Morning Fun Club is like being in a sea shell, with the roaring of water sound inside and all around you, pushing you crazily from one activity to another, too rushed to notice who's a friend, everybody is. The best activity is trampoline. On trampoline I can do the swivel hips.

For Saturday Morning Fun Club you also learn to sneak out in the lunch slot of your colour and go around the corner to Nut and Candy Land. You buy whatever you want from trays piled with sculpted chocolate and colourfully wrapped candies behind a glass counter. It doesn't mean anything to the ladies behind the counter where you came from, around the corner. They don't care there's no grown up with you. They wear white button-up dresses. They let you pick what you want and they put it in a little brown paper bag.

With sunflower seeds if someone tells you to put them all in your mouth and just eat them like that, don't. You should take the shells off first. But in my opinion sunflower seeds are not worth it. All the time it takes to get the shell off for that little amount of seed is way too much work. Turkish delight, what Edmund got from the witch in Narnia, is really not worth all that he went through either.

There's a naked feeling of going to the candy store but the naked feeling is in your ears, in the rush of cars and the busy jostling people on the sidewalk, all bigger but none yours so no protection. So what they said in the newspaper about Selena being sick so not in swim class and not getting the regular supervision was true but also beside the point. You could do whatever you wanted to if you wanted to at the Y. It wasn't jail. Anyone could.

The lunchroom for Saturday Morning Fun Club is the All Purpose Room. Hot, with so many girls in it, you need to open the windows even in winter. Coming back from Nut and Candy Land, I get a seat at a crowded table and try to come up with a strategy to deal with getting the shells off my sunflower seeds. Brita's there, smiling; she compliments me on my t-shirt. I'm wearing it again.

TEN

People want an answer. They look at me shocked Selena was only ten. Then it's my job to explain, it's my responsibility because of who I am, because when you hear a girl is only ten you assume she isn't sexually developed yet. But Selena was already. She was. She was—I heard my mom say.

There's nothing wrong, when you say it, of adding an insinuating tone or a sneer, almost of knowing a deeper meaning to her being that way. You don't have to take the explanation any further. Even when what he did to her was so bad and so terrible and can never be undone you're still allowed to say it that way. It's good enough.

Like being that way was Selena's fault, what she did wrong, for attracting Cal. Not a fault she could be blamed for, just a fault.

AFTER PRACTICE

After morning practice Bruce Ferguson and I steer ourselves squinting like moles, hair steaming and beginning to freeze from the wetness of our swim still there, eyes burning and red from two hours in too much chlorine, through the bright morning, to my mom's steaming green Cortina. It's got the normal car exhaust but exaggeratedly steamy from the cold, and the windows are misted up from the ventilation system not working properly and the condensation freezing not only on the outside of the windows but on the inside too. So when mom is driving she frantically attacks different frosted-up sections on the inside of the window with her scraper at stoplights.

Adding to the steaminess is mom and Lana, sitting in the front smoking their sweet-smelling mentholated Cameo cigarettes. They turn their heads towards us in unison when we get in the back seat, Lana with her happy dopey smile, like they've just returned from their mother ship and its alien atmosphere. They smoke so many cigarettes that the ashtray is overflowing and smoking too. It's like the ashtray is another special friend of their secret society and is joining in, enjoying its own cigarette.

If I breathe through my mouth with small shallow breaths I avoid knowing the sweet stench, which it's easy to do because I already am to avoid the ache that's in my lungs from the chlorine.

Lana's job is at London Life, right across the street from the Y. She just has to get out of the car and walk over when she's ready. First she touches mom lightly on the wrist like she's about to say something important but forgot, so has to give her a special affectionate look to compensate.

Lana has a smile in her eye. Even the way she walks is funny. The way she walks is like any minute she might make a funny little skip in the air like Red Skelton the clown used to on his TV show. And when she does we'll hear the ring-a-ling cowbell sound that always accompanied it too.

The green Cortina is my mom's first car all her own. It only cost four hundred dollars or something. Besides its suspect air ventilation system, its springs are shot and the interior of the ceiling caves in on your head when it's stressed, which it always is when you go over bumps, because of the bad suspension. When that happens you just have to push it back up in its place.

By the time we get to Kipps Lane, which is more like an old bumpy country road than a city street, leading to our subdivision, the car is bounding up and down like a boat on a rocky ocean so that we can't keep up with pushing the ceiling back in its place. Bruce and I are looking at each other laughing because it's like a crazy ride that's out of control and mom is laughing with us too.

5

THE BUS

The other way of getting home after swim practice is the bus. Waiting for the first bus at Dundas and Wellington there's no one special. Buses going straight through without stopping kick up slush so you need to stand away, close to the building, until it's the right one. The transfer at Adelaide is the first regular, the kid with the long scraggly hair, soft freckles and looking up sideways face.

His tilting look starts at the bottom because his legs don't straighten all the way. So he uses the wall he's leaning against and metal crutches, the short kind with the ring you put your arms through, going right under his armpits and then a handle part farther down, to prop him up. His spot is the southeast corner waiting, under the Credit Union sign. Seeing him I always feel like I'm floating in heaven on earth. That there's this soft light connected through everyone.

That he and I are connected on a special level only it's not one of those where you're in love with the person and it's deep and romantic or that I even think he's this guy with these very special insights because of the sad way that he is. In fact, I think something is wrong with him, besides his body, his eyes drifting off.

Seeing him, I feel like God put him there for some reason I can't figure out. Like he's not even a real person with a real life he's living, like he's a prop for me. I don't feel guilty or bad about it either, like my thinking it, which isn't really fair, is taking away his chance of having a real life. I just wonder why God would connect us like that.

Only I already figured out a while ago that God is just for people who don't have the stamina to handle that there isn't a God.

NICE PEOPLE

Sometimes our parents would take us to a non-denominational church, which is believing in God any way you want, at the end of a long back road lined with trees with a parking lot made of white stones that sparkle.

One time I made cutout children with their hands joining. Another time an older girl showed me how to tie up my shoelaces the easy way so then I could tie up my shoes. Everyone is so nice. I've never been in a place that so consistently oozed such niceness.

Going to church is sporadic, a few spats of going to church, then we don't go anymore. Then we try again later, at a different non-denominational church downtown, the same routine. I don't know if my dad minds it so much. He enjoys the socializing. It's my mom I think it's more upsetting for because of the waiting, the waiting for the other shoe to drop, for the nice masks to come off when she doesn't want to keep agreeing with everything they say about the nice way it is anymore.

There's a picture in Sunday school class of Jesus, stern but gentle-faced in soft-hued red and blue robes with lines showing light emanating from his body to the sky. Or maybe it's the other way around and the light is coming down from the sky to his body.

Light like that coming off your body for all to see would make a slightly spooky whirring sound.

WORD

At the Adelaide bus stop there's also the word. It's the word OPEECHEE and it runs down the length of a yellow brick building. Its letters are in white against a black background. It's for the O-Pee-Chee bubble gum factory.

Ladies covering up white uniforms with winter coats scurry on thick-calved, beige-stockinged legs in and out of the building. Different days they're making different sickly sweet bubble-gum-flavoured smells emanating through the neighbourhood.

WHERE NOT TO SIT

After the transfer, the second bus home, it's the high schoolers from Sir George Ross, which is for kids who can't get into regular high school because they're not smart enough so they go there to learn cooking and shop. The leader of the group doesn't act sad about not going to a good school. She's a black girl with a big afro so we're the same because of having the same style of hair.

She's the leader because she's always talking animatedly, touching the other kids when they're lucky enough for it to be their turn. Exuberant and loud, which I can be too, only not here on the bus with no one I know. I am just quietly watching from the side, which is how I am more turning into being in regular life too.

Alone on the bus, moving, I don't feel sad about it. I like watching the jovial black girl joke with her friends. I feel connected, not even in a weird "Is there a God?" kind of way.

Since I'm sitting in the seat just in front of the rear door exit when they're piling off at the stop for their school, she pats my big fluffy-hair head on the way out—a jolt of otherness—her next peal of laughter dampened by the bus's closing doors.

GRADE FOUR

Lori Newton is taking her clothes off and getting naked right in front of Mrs. Tobias. The reason is because it's June and school is almost done. When it's June and you're in grade four at our school you get to go on a school bus to swim lessons for a week, first thing after lunch, instead of regular classes.

Whereas I'm normal. I change in the little change stalls in the locker room behind the plastic curtains hanging on the metal hooks, put there for that purpose.

Since I've never had swim lessons before I'm put with the group of kids that don't know how to swim who are getting ignored and am stuck with them the whole week in the shallow end with no instruction and no one even noticing I know how to swim already. I'm very good.

It gives mom the idea of sending us to take swim and diving lessons and join the swim team and the diving team all summer. Plus hanging out at the pool for free swim too.

GOLDEN

Then every Wednesday night we go to the Twilight Swim Meet and I win gold first-place ribbons every time. Mom gets me a gold sweat suit the same colour as the ribbons and the twilight to keep me from getting cold in between races because she whispers to me I might be able to join the London Y Aquatic Club and their team colours are green and gold, but don't tell anyone, it's a secret.

The sweat suit is a strange-looking gold, a brown gold, not a bright one that looks even more brown-coloured when it gets wet. The part that gets wettest is the bum from sitting with your wet bathing suit on underneath. Mom gets Cal a green sweat suit for the same reason, but it's more of a normal-looking green, even though he's not as good as me at winning swim races.

I don't know why it's a secret. Won't people look at us and the colours we're wearing and figure out the code of what it is we're planning?

SHANNON WILLIAMS

Shannon's mom is nicer than mine. Shannon juggles better than me no matter how much I practice. She knows which rain boots are the more fashionable and tells me mine are the wrong kind after I beg my mom to get me ones like hers but they turn out not to be for some detail I didn't notice, trying to get close to being like her. Her mom and Bruce Ferguson's talk about how cute they are together, like a couple. Nadia Petakov, an older girl who lives on our street, treats only Shannon special, taking her on hikes down in the valley. Shannon has straight long strawberry blond hair. She's cute. She is nice. Tammy Gilbert isn't mean to her when she's teacher when we play school. She doesn't have to write the initials C.P. on her hand for cootie proof because nobody ever says she has them.

I tell her how good of a swimmer I am, all my ribbons, but I could just be bragging. It could be not real. We're in the Gilberts' swimming pool so I'm going to show her by racing her. It's not that I want to beat her to show her. Well, I would like that too.

I really wonder whether I can beat her. On one side, she's better than me in everything. On the other, nobody can beat me at swimming.

MAGIC

I wasn't the one picked by the magician. He picked a different girl, a nice regular one, only she was too scared. I didn't give her time to maybe stop being that way. Someone could have beaten me to it. I put up my hand and said I would be the helper.

Instead of the cake I was helping him bake in three seconds, it was a magic white baby bunny. Then my parents were nodding I could keep it and I was the girl with the magic bunny and dad made a hutch for it to live in when we got home.

AIR

Even though I'm such a good swimmer I'm also really afraid. I don't understand why I am, just like I don't understand why I'm such a good swimmer. We're playing in the water at the beach. I'm under the water in the shadow of an air mattress which I will not swim underneath.

What if I'm trying to get up for air and the mattress gets in my way and I'm pushing to get up and the mattress with the person's body on it is pressing down on me and I can't get to the air?

TUCKED AWAY

Mom is friends with Ross's mom when we're in Bayfield. His dad is swim coach at the university. Their cottage has the kind of spruces out front that make the big skirts at the bottom you can hide under and bring your toys and make yourself a special little protected, tucked-away house.

We're with Ross under there while our mom is in the house with his mom. She's helping. It's about his dad and his drinking.

END OF THE LINE

Since I'm swimming and taking the bus, Cindy is getting the job of looking after the bunnies mostly. We don't have mine from the magician anymore. It died. Then one day my mom was in the Market Building and she saw two other really cute bunnies and it was so perfect she had to bring them home, one for Cindy and one for me. Matching. Like how she used to like to buy us matching clothes, but in different colours, sometimes.

THE WALKWAYS

Except Cindy and I don't match at all. That's why my mom buying us matching clothes isn't as obnoxious as it sounds. Cindy is very small and cute. I am very big and not cute. She is practically always the teacher's favourite. I never am.

One time we were walking along the walkways, the ones right in front of where my teacher from when I was in kindergarten lives, and she said to me, "It takes me two steps to your one when we're walking."

I knew she was just saying it to remind me of how adorable she is compared to me. Why else would she say something so completely untrue? I don't take especially big steps when I walk. I don't. In fact, I admire people who do. I'm just not one of them. And she's not the baby-step walker type either. Horrid and petite as she is, she doesn't have an itsy-bitsy mincing walk.

SAME LOCATION

Two other things happened at that same spot on the walkways where Cindy was reminding me of how cute she was.

The first thing that happened is my best friend Julie Pollard's very mean older sister told me I was a freak and to stop staring at her. The second is it was the place where I found out, by one of my friends telling me, about how sex works, about the boy putting his penis into the girl.

FURTHER CORRELATIONS

Which exactly coincided with my finding out that my teacher, Mrs. Penelope, from kindergarten, the one living right at the end of the walkway, was pregnant and about to have a baby. Mrs. Penelope! Mrs. Penelope who would always be talking in a nice voice when the problem with me was my voice was too big. My body was too big. My fingers were too big.

The fresh air on me after going outside to recess didn't get off me fast enough so that I could put myself back properly into being in kindergarten and the job of playing exactingly with the teacups in the dollhouse, extracting—fingers like tweezers—the money out of the bright pinging cash register.

How could someone so upright as Mrs. Penelope, someone having such a feeling for and commitment to correcting how wrong everything was about me, get herself involved in such crazy shenanigans as penises and the innie girl part?

CLOSED

Then every time I'm going by the exact same spot on the walkways on the way home from school, I'm trying to figure out how Mrs. Penelope is going to get from her regular perfect self to the putting in the penis part with her husband, Mr. Penelope, a nice smiley, square-headed, stay in the background person not minding being all tidy in the corner of her perfection.

Every time I go by, her house is never open. No one is gardening even though the flower bed looks fine. It looks perfect, just like her. After the baby comes, she doesn't leave the stroller out on the front porch. She doesn't leave the front door open so the breeze can blow through the screen door when the weather turns nice.

Like she's hiding her head in shame.

THIS MORNING

It's always mom's emotions that take over. When I get home from swim practice she's wailing the tragic news, dramatic and important, like the acceptance speech of winning an award. At the same time she's deftly making sure not to forget Cindy. Since it was Cindy it really happened to.

She keeps circling back to the Bouviers, how Bouvier dogs came up from the valley. That's who did it. She's going to find out who the dogs belong to if it's the only thing she does. Bouviers are bad dogs.

PERMISSION

It's like mom gives herself permission to feel all these things but we're not allowed. It's like her feelings are the only ones that it's safe for us to feel.

DISAPPEARING ACT

I don't even like these bunnies anyway. The one that's been designated as Cindy's is kind of cute. He stretches up to you and touches you with his wiggly rabbit nose. He puts up his ears to listen. But mine is plain afraid. It skulks in corners and doesn't come out.

When I had my rabbit from the magician he was big and friendly and cuddly. He was song-worthy, story-worthy. I resent the implications that Cindy's bunny is the cuter, friendlier one and that mine's a dud.

STREWN

Mom says how sad it is Cindy had to see it, which is putting them together again, mom and Cindy. I get left imagining the ripped-open rabbit hutch, the torn-up rabbit corpses. Imagine our pets' fear, how they would have acted. Imagine Cindy's morning trek to the hutch at the bottom of the yard, her dipping around the heavy snow-covered pine branches, interrupted. Bloody snow. Bodies strewn. Pink innards.

Like the picture in the newspaper of the stairwell at the Y where they found the body the next morning. But including the body. Even if it's only our pet animal bodies.

GRIEF

I don't know why mom's allowing it. Why does she think we deserve to join in the grieving? If it's not Cal's fault because he's crazy—if it won't be mom's or dad's fault because it had to be each other's and it won't land—then whose fault is it?

Who's going to say they're sorry?

What I do is my job. It's my job to go back and forth to swim practice to show it was just an accident, to show how normal our family really is, to be responsible.

6

LUNCH

Mom makes a plan for us to eat lunch at Shannon Williams' who has a younger sister the same age as Cindy, so we're not sad about the rabbits, at home eating lunch by ourselves. Shannon's mom, with her nice normal-coloured hair, Mrs. Williams, is making us Kraft Dinner for lunch, even though I could be making my own Kraft Dinner at home by myself. Shannon is showing respect for the situation by not informing me like last time I was here I'm wrong for liking putting catsup on it.

The atmosphere is sickly sweet like how garbage smells

when it keeps being forgotten to be taken out. It's in my stomach, my head, in my chest the sickly ache of—please let me out of here—like maybe I'm going to die from suffocation if somebody doesn't let me up for air soon. Unfortunately, because of my swim training, I'm really good at holding my breath for long periods of time.

I get that it's what my sister needs. I do. I just don't know how they do it, her and mom. I heard what we're supposed to do. We're supposed to be taking care of it all by ourselves. I'm fine. I can do it. I've got the stamina. How do they change the rules like that?

THUNDERSTORMS

Our mom was really afraid of thunderstorms but we weren't. She had all these things about it, like stay away from the window or else the lightning will come in and get you.

Maybe because she was so scared it felt like fun for us for a change. The crabapple tree was mom too, because it had beautiful orangey red apples in the fall like her hair and soft pink blossoms in the spring because it reminded you she was still beautiful even if she wouldn't let herself be. And the name—crabapple: what a crabby mom we had!

One time the storm was close to ending and we were ready to go out with our bathing suits on into the street to run through the puddles while they were still big, but she wasn't ready for the storm to be over yet. That was when Cindy went out and was running around and around the crabapple tree. Mom was yelling at her to come back in the house and would have run out there after her and snatched her up in her arms if she was able to think of it—if she wasn't so paralyzed from being afraid.

WANT

What I want is a bra. I know my breasts aren't very big but I wish my mom would let me have a bra. I don't want to be a disappointment to her though. There are so many things I know I'm not supposed to want, to be good enough to be the person she needs me to be.

GUY FROM CAL'S CLASS

This is the kid at the bottom rung of the ladder, even lower than Cal. Because Cal was small and was the kid that got moved from the smart class to the dumb class in grade five, he was towards the bottom. Because Cal was scared of the big boys and intimidated but then couldn't help but open his big mouth and say what he was thinking making them madder, he was towards the bottom.

When Cal turned out good at trumpet, you could expect something like that, but it still didn't change his ranking.

Like Beverly Talbot in my class. Thick glasses, monkey mouth. Whatever you do, don't be associated with that girl. She never didn't have cooties. But then when Sheila Sears moved to the school, it was hard to tell. She was such a liar but sometimes you were convinced. It was difficult to get what her ranking was.

With Annie Windsor, who was in Cal's grade, she would keep finding ways of approaching me after and saying how she thought about him all the time. She thought about what happened. She could never believe it of him because he wasn't like that. He was sweet and nice. And of how much she always liked him. Then she would do it again. She'd say something different but it would be the same. How she liked him so much and had wished for him to be her boyfriend, only you could tell she still wished for it now. She was still wishing for it.

The bottom-rung guy is small too, like Cal, and carrying a paper-route bag over his shoulder, with the long kind of hair that's parted on the side so he's always swinging it back up in a long face.

He's saying, "Your being the sister means you're just like him, aren't you?" And more like that, when he sees me. Taunting. Except it would be pretty stupid of him to say that to me if I really was like that, wouldn't it? His saying it makes me want to be it, what he says, a lot.

It's easy to make it not happen. All I have to do is avoid him so that he can't say it to me. But he's always around with that paper-route bag and that idea in his head.

SWIM TIP #2—BREATHING IN

At the beginning of joining a swim team, the pool water, which started out still and calm without six lanes of ten kids per lane swimming in six long skinny circles, feels rough. There's a lot of water going down your throat and up your nose in a way you don't want.

For the mouth part, it's the opposite of what you think. Don't stretch your head way out of the water to avoid the waves. That will only increase the chances of getting more water down your throat. The top of the wave is the most unpredictable. It's the worst place to try to get air.

If you keep your mouth close to the surface of the water, tilting your head only slightly, the way your body floats on the water top will make sure there's a nice pocket of air there for you right at the surface of wherever it is your body's got to in the water, trough or crest.

Don't suck the air in too quickly because even tucked in so snug to the water's surface, there can be turbulent moments. Then if there's a problem you'll have enough time to make an adjustment, to stop your breathing in and not accidentally suck in more water.

EVERY OTHER YEAR

There's pictures in the school hallway from every other year of grade eight graduates, lined up in rows, squinting and smiling in the sunshine in front of the school. I don't know how the principal and grade eight teachers get convinced but they give Alan Schmidt, a student in our class, the job of taking the graduation picture.

Alan Schmidt doesn't know how to use the benches and line the rows up properly but they just let him not know. Since I'm tall, in the tall row, I'm standing right behind people whose heads are covering up most of my face. Everyone in my row has to decide whether to peek our faces around or over, by standing on tiptoes, the heads in front of ours. Or not.

Also there isn't going to be a formal dance this year. So we don't get to wear special clothes and we don't get to maybe, if someone asks us, go on first dates, since my parents would have to let me go to my own graduation dance, wouldn't they? Instead there's a pool party with hamburgers and chips at the Panners'.

When my teacher Mr. Whalen does a cannonball from the diving board I find out he has a soft flabby tummy and a chest that's flabby too, like with small breasts. In his suits he always looks like he's skinny. Now I realize I should have noticed better the way his neck and his chin went, sticking out from the top of the suit. If I'd paid better attention I wouldn't have been surprised by how he looks underneath.

AROUND

It's like if anything goes my way, if I get anything I want, like a normal graduation picture, I might turn into a crazy sex fiend too. So everybody's working around this possibility.

If this is true it's really nice of everybody to put aside their needs and do this for me, to give me a chance to be normal like everyone else.

THE REASON MOON

Even if the moon has no atmosphere and is full of craters, the fact it pulls the earth's ocean's waters towards it causing tides makes it seem alive. It's part of us even if it seems so far away and different and inaccessible. If you imagine the ocean without tides it practically wouldn't even be an ocean anymore, it would just be a big boring placid lake.

The reason the moon is a woman and your mother and one day you is because of its pulling power. Your mother pulls you into doing things for her all the time. Like being a great swimmer. Like not being a problem. The reason there's a man in the moon is the man represents men getting sucked up into her.

When man landed on the moon he was all "Aren't I the greatest with my rocket power and my engineering." But maybe in actuality getting there was just another example of the pulling power of the moon.

VISIT

Mom and dad are mostly talking to him. We're in a long corridor with high ceilings and glass windows that make it bright with lots of panes in them. The panes make it look homey like the Christmas cards that have the cute little red brick houses also with the windows with the panes, but with the snow nestled in the separating parts of the panes too.

There's a wicker picnic basket with special things including a jar of Klondike dad made him. Klondike is this special sandwich spread he makes that Cal loves. It's dad's way of showing he still loves him and that's what we're all here showing.

Dad always wants to be everybody's best friend so it makes sense that he makes him the Klondike. It's also brave for him to keep caring. Because a psychopath with no feelings is dangerous, isn't it? Because of what he did. Remember?

CINDY

Also before it happened, Cindy was attacked at home by him, she thinks, only she went unconscious when it happened. It's between her and mom.

WHAT HAPPENED TO ME

The only thing I can think of is the time the kids in the neighbourhood were giving me a pink-belly, which is where they make quick little slaps on your tummy until it goes red. I don't usually get myself in those kinds of situations because of being big and resisting, facing them down if they try. It's just I told them they could do it at first not realizing how much it was going to hurt. My stomach is very sensitive.

I was crying for them to stop, it was hurting so bad. I was trapped and couldn't get myself free. And Cal was there, and he looked at me looking at him pleading for him to make them stop, and it went on for this while, me looking him in the eye, begging, and him looking me in mine, considering, and then it clicked, and he told them to stop.

Only now I don't know if the click was about he cared about me or if the click was if he didn't get them to set me free, I would tell on him and mom would be mad.

JUST IN CASE

If you're scared of who Cal may have turned into all you should do is make sure to always give in to him and what he wants. If you just always give in to him he'll always stay innocent because there'll never be something he can't get from you. Never resist him and what he wants.

Watch his eyes. Let him talk first. Answer politely.

ANOTHER TIME

One time my sister wouldn't leave me alone. We were in the basement in the playroom. Finally I just grabbed her arms and pressed her, crushed her, to the floor with all my body strength, like I was Frankenstein. I didn't care about getting in trouble. I was just so sick of her needing and being all over me.

DIFFERENT

Cal looks completely different. His voice changed because of when boys go through puberty their voices get deeper. It's from his chest. Before, even though he was already sixteen, his voice was still the same, reasonable like a sweet sing-song songbird. Now if it wasn't him it would be like a wolf you saw growling in an animal trap.

Also his hair turned very thick and curly when it was mostly straight before. His eyes got very droopy-looking. That, combined with the tone in the new voice, makes him seem even more like one of us, because of how much what he's turned into somehow reminds me of Aunt Sylvia, my mom's sister.

He liked the drive up to Penetanguishene because the police driving him were speeding the whole way. He's smiling, thinking of that.

7

BEST FRIEND

My best friend Julie Pollard is finally getting to escape her mean older sister, the meanest ever, only Julie never complains; she admires her. Julie's coming with me to Central High School, which is downtown.

For me it will be easier since I train for swimming at the downtown Y in the morning so after I'll just walk to school a few blocks. Also at night we're training at Wolseley Barracks now, a military base, which isn't that far away either. I'm going to walk there after school.

BEAUTIFUL

Central High School is much more beautiful than Montcalm, the high school in my home neighbourhood. Central is surrounded by trees. It has an architectural style—Edwardian. Across the street is Dr. Peter Hoffman's office, who used to be the head coach of the London Y Aquatic Club only now he's too old.

It has downtown and Victoria Park and City Hall nearby. Also my mom's store is just across the street from the park.

To get to Montcalm you have to take a crosswalk over a road that on the one side is a country highway on its way up and out of a valley and on the other side is a big city street on its way to the mall. Then after you cross the crosswalk with the traffic coming up the hill at you that you can't see until the last minute, you have to walk up more of a hill, up the steps to get to Montcalm.

I know all the other kids do it but thinking of going to that school makes me think of getting hit by a car.

It's where Cal was going.

CHASING TENNIS BALLS

Before we were in high school Julie invited me to come to Montcalm with her in the summer and play tennis on the tennis courts. There was no one else around, but it was so hot with no trees over the court and I think Julie was an awful tennis player. We just kept hitting the balls at each other and then the other person wouldn't be able to hit it back, either because it wasn't anywhere close to them or because they couldn't hit it back.

I hate being too hot with no shade. The bright light pushing so hard on you, your eyes squeeze shut from feeling the darkness in too much light.

POLLUTION

That's what Julie is like. She'll get these ideas in her head for adventures and then just go do them, only once you're there, there can be this stillness of boredom and not being able to handle being there, not knowing what to do.

Another time her idea was that we needed to clean up the pollution in the creek in the valley. That was the first time we almost became best friends. So we were down in the creek moving twigs and branches around that were blocking water and allowing white suds from the pollution-causing phosphates to build up. At least I think that's what we were doing.

The good thing was then we went for a walk in the valley, exploring. We found an old fallen-down tree with no bark on it but that was still exciting to climb on top of and survey the surroundings from a position of power. We found an entire forest of small pine trees in rows with big yellow grass tufts in between that you could lie down on, in the warm and still, and hide from enemies.

Then we were passing the actually not very polluted-looking creek and exploring the valley a few times.

But Julie said she couldn't be best friends with me because she was already best friends with Donna Snowden so then I wouldn't be friends with her anymore because it wasn't good enough for me.

REALIZE

What I should have realized was Donna Snowden was really the mentally retarded girl living across the street from Julie. How I figured this out eventually was how come Donna Snowden didn't go to our school? Also, how come despite being best friends Julie actually hardly played with Donna Snowden?

Why it made sense for so long was I thought Donna must be someone so absolutely special I could never be invited to play with her. Like a princess.

That was how we would knock heads because Julie always stood up for her principles, especially her loyalty to the downtrodden, even if they were completely incomprehensible and she didn't tell you what they were.

OATS

After a while Julie and I got to be best friends again without saying it. Then Julie was reading to me the letter she was writing to another older sister, one who is nice to her and away at university, and in it she's telling her sister how we are best friends. So that's like Julie's gift of letting me know she remembers and her concession of admitting what I wanted is true but in a sweet subtle kind of way.

It's a spring Sunday, a warm one melting the snow. My mom is helping us make oat delights, which is a kind of cookie that you just make, you don't have to cook, only we have to go to Julie's to get some more oats.

We're funny because we're running and skipping to

her house reciting the poem "The Charge of the Light Brigade," only it isn't cannons to the left and right, it's oats.

We are having so much fun that my mom lets me skip afternoon swim practice. She's not saying anything about it though. She's just letting it happen.

ONLY

Except mom and Julie are so into their conversation, which is pretty awesome, right? Showing how valuable they both are and proving how great I am since in a way they're both mine. I'm trying to get in on the cool way they are together, like when I found out Cal was good at joking and so I wanted to be too. Only Cal's not here anymore.

I'm okay with Julie. I'm already on the inside of Julie liking me but I'm on the outside of mom and Julie liking each other because of Julie's having the four older brothers and sisters and feeling like the last and least. So you can see how the knowing of all those things, not only making up her own Dr. Seuss-like poems when she was only in grade three, but more, made her get so smart and ahead of herself and sad because of it too.

But with me, all there supposedly is is the fact of how cool and funny a mother I have, including the evidence of how Julie and her are laughing and getting along so well. Consequently because of the greatness of my mom I can't possibly know what it is they know together. Plus it's important for my mom that I stay the way I am, not having problems with her, for my own protection. Like not smoking cigarettes.

I like the getting out of swim practice for a change but Julie and mom's talking to each other the whole time is like the rectangular prism shape that is the Bob Hayward Y swimming pool, the Y we train at on Sundays, floating in the air of the kitchen.

It's attached to the string that is the drive along Highbury Avenue, past Julie's house, the Kmart then farther to the bridge over the tracks at Dundas looking over where the Salvation Army houses are which is where I want to be.

It's where I used to want to be. Five or six neat red brick houses you can see from above like ant hills because of the bridge view, which is the same as how God must be looking down on them because of their never doubting being his religion. Only when I used to want that I didn't know where places were by directions yet, and so I couldn't predict when they would sneak up on me, with their desire to be somewhere not here, not so compliant, not so high-pitched, somewhere it was going to be okay to be believing something different, somewhere more organized and with the feeling of being cared for.

Sally's at the end of the string, my coach, pulling the other kids through their laps for two hours, wondering where I am. And the knowing I have of my mom explaining something to her later, and of her being accountable.

So the whole while we're making cookies it's like I'm attached to that string of swimming up and down the pool for two hours anyway, which is why I don't like spring. Everything is new so you think you're getting out of something but the wetness and the cold are still there like a swimming pool heaved out of the ground hovering in the air, weighing on and reminding you.

ALSO

The other reason for going to Central is that Yvonne Nowak, Angela White and Louise Miles from the swim team are all going to Central too.

WHO I HANG OUT WITH

Julie and I get no classes the same and lunches opposite too. It's the same with Yvonne Nowak. Louise Miles wouldn't hang out with me at school anyway because she's already in grade eleven.

If she went by standards of school friends Louise wouldn't even consider hanging out with Yvonne and me after morning swim practice at the cafeteria at the Y eating toast and making us feel like we like and want to eat toast too.

For how to pick friends at Central I'm emulating Louise Miles whose best friend is Talia Bevan, top female athlete of the school plus so socially involved having time to organize the annual girls' sleepover in the gym, which because of her I actually talked my mom into letting me go to. Talia is so athletic. She is shorter than Louise with big calf muscles that sprout out angularly like rhombus quadrilaterals below her knee-length skirts. They spread up her body and into her face flexed in an always-smiling muscle.

Louise and Talia eat lunch in the cafeteria together along with other girlfriends in their group also having significant accomplishments like talking about being on important committees and always having books to study in their arms.

PARTNER

My homeroom is biology and I get Jesse McIntyre for lab partner, a girl, even though some Jesses are boys. Jesse has soft green eyes and light red hair, a turned-up nose but not snobby, and a little bit of a sway back but not the girly soft and giggly kind, more the girly perfect sway back, so that when she looks at the teacher that sway is in her eyes and it goes right down to the soul of her perfect do everything right, straight as an arrow, except sways aren't straight, perfectness.

I'm not saying I don't like her. I'd like to like her. It's just she doesn't really notice me, but not in a snobby way. She seems tired.

LUNCH

For sitting in the cafeteria at lunch I get in with Sarah Longman, Trudy Jensen, Angela McCormick who are similar to Louise's group only in my grade. They come from the same grade school even.

The reason it works out my being allowed with them is the tacit agreement we have I won't try to get in with them all the way. Which how could I? I have swim practice.

Sometimes I can tell that Sarah Longman may actually despise me though. She gets this look in her short but curly thick eyelashes eyes of, "I really don't know you and what you say doesn't prove much either." But it's just a look.

Since I don't come from one of the grade schools that come automatically to Central, Sarah Longman is right, nobody does know who I am. Or do they? There's two things they could have heard about me.

The second thing is—I am such a good swimmer.

COUNTING RIGHT

Louise Miles always counts right. We do a lot of "thousand" sets. Forty lengths then rest. Another forty lengths. So Louise is swimming behind you, going slower, maybe you're even going to lap her making you over two lengths ahead of her and you finish your forty lengths, touch the wall, put your feet on the ledge, catch your breath and Louise is there already. You counted wrong. That's what she says.

Since she's so smart I believe her. And so does Hanley Bell, Travis Bauman, Yvonne, everyone. Only it keeps happening.

INSIDE NUMBERS

When you're inside a thousand you're doing the number forty. After one length you're one fortieth finished but after two lengths you're one twentieth, which amazingly is twice as good. But twice as good can be defeating because then you have to do that entire amount, twice as much, to get to the next major fraction with a number one at the front, which is one tenth.

After one tenth of the way through you get looking ahead to how much farther you have to go to get to one half, one out of two, which is the final destination of having a number one at the front half of the equation but when you get there you're still only halfway done.

The best number of doing a thousand is twenty-six. Actually it's twenty-seven. Because at twenty-six you're well past halfway done and at twenty-seven you're ecstatically past halfway. But when you get to twenty-eight it's not better anymore because by then you're only back to the work of finishing three hundred more metres of the pool to go.

It's harder than you think to hold on to the numbers, which is why it's easy to be uncertain and believe Louise. If you hold on to them too hard you can change the number too early, before you get to the end of the length of the pool, so when you do your flip turn you're not sure anymore did it get changed already.

There's also the question of what happens to the numbers in your head when you do your flip turn—do the numbers flip upside down and turn over too and the sticks of the numbers knock into each other falling down on their sides reminding you of how when you were a kid falling down playing dead you always had to have your arms and legs spread out in an X in the dead-man position or you didn't feel properly dead, the numbers confusing themselves into other numbers, especially because while you're flipping the number's going up one digit too.

Or do they float like in little bubbles, accommodated by the bubble, which does the spinning, so the number can stay upright the whole time and keep track of itself better.

MORE SMART THINGS ABOUT LOUISE

Sometimes you'll go with a different family to a swim meet. This time Louise Miles is coming with our family to a swim meet in Montreal. We're staying at my Aunt Sylvia's who lives in an apartment building and has an outdoor and an indoor swimming pool and a waterbed. She's on her second husband.

Louise invented a game where first you say something and then the other person says something completely unrelated back, like that, back and forth. Try it. It's really hard to think of something completely new that has nothing to do with what the person said right before and then keep doing it.

Unfortunately it's making my Aunt Sylvia feel on the outside even though she's clearly cool because she's smart herself and has a university degree and speaks French and English and teaches high school. What upsets her most is when she finds the bathing cap in the freezer. That was just because we also have two imaginary pet snakes, Suzette and Herman, Louise's idea too, who were in the bathing cap and were hot and wanted to go in the freezer.

Then my mom has to explain to her what good kids we really are.

PINK WARTS

Then when we're at the swim meet, Louise introduces me to Luke Humphries who swims for Pointe Claire, which is a really good team with lots of national champions and team members and Luke is one of them in the two hundred breaststroke, with gorgeous skin all over his body like a wall of it, sweet brown eyes like chocolate kisses, really, and blond hair that poufs up at the front even though it's straight.

She just made friends with him. Like that. Then they're playing knuckles, which is where you face each other and line up your hands downwards facing in fists and try to rap their knuckles with yours but they're not allowed to move their hands until you move yours.

Louise gets me to do that with him too. Except—oh no— the warts. Because I have these warts on my hands. They are so gross that my best friend Julie Pollard from grade eight, but who's not my best friend anymore, came up with the idea for me to give them names. Then she helped me make up a combination of silly and classy names for them so I would feel better about having them.

Also I put pink nail polish on them, which is half coming off from all the swimming because the wart-kill stuff doesn't work and someone told me nail polish would suffocate them.

I would never talk to Luke on my own anyway. Most swimmers have the really big chest muscles but Luke's, along with that kind of beautiful skin he has on them, are even bigger. Even though he turns out so friendly, his voice so warm and letting you in despite his gorgeousness, not even disgusted by the warts and liking their funny names and not coming on all flirty and scary either, I still would never talk to him on my own without Louise there.

It's not just that I know knowing a boy like that would be a problem for what my family needs, a boy you like for being a boy, a boy you think about wanting to like you. But from my own self I wouldn't know if they felt trustworthy. How do you know who is going to be trustworthy? I think the answer is no one.

WHERE

What would I do with a boy if I brought one home anyway? How would I explain his purpose to my mom? There wouldn't be any purpose he could have. Maybe he would find out things about us he wasn't supposed to. He would just get in the way. He would be useless.

HEADING HOME

My best friend Julie and I are riding the bus home together. The problem is our schedules have changed so we can start being together more at school only I still want to be with my new group, the girls from north London. Julie's not interested in being with them and doesn't even have to say it. Besides she wouldn't know how you have to be to be with them. They wouldn't want her either anyway. Why should I have to give them up to be with Julie?

Julie's friends aren't popular. I don't know who they are. Julie plays flute and now she's added playing bassoon. Her parents pay for private lessons. Julie's friends are probably other kids in the school band, people on the side. Clammy, needy, overweight. I'm not even interested in band.

We get off the bus and are walking towards our homes. Julie's telling me to fuck off, but she doesn't really say it like she means it, which is what I'm against about her. That's what I'm arguing with her about. Say it like you mean it, is what I say. She tries but she still says it like how sad she is, how she just wants to give up, how she just wishes I wouldn't be abandoning her like that, like the way everyone else always does in her family.

But for me the point is, when you say fuck off, you should say it like you mean it.

8

PILED ON

What my dad does with the new coach from Australia is get me there late for the first swim practice. Dad's so mad about how the board of the club treated Sally the old coach because the older boys don't respect her because she's a woman. Only what he does, with mom, is tell me it's all a good thing and how good it will be for me to have a world-class coach. Then I say that to Sally, before she's done with being our coach, and her eyes get all big and hurt in betrayed shock so I realize dad didn't tell her what it was he was planning on telling me.

Going through the shower room at the Y, it has those signs up saying, "Please be sure to wash yourself with soap before you enter the pool." No one would do that at six in the morning. Especially because of how much worse it would make the icky, clammy journey from the locker room to the pool.

Before leaving the shower area, which is where Cal was sneaking into and feeling up some women's bodies but they didn't realize it was him yet, you go up some tile stairs through a heavy steel door in case of fire, to a dingy hallway with one of those black slip-free rubber runners so as not to trip with the little stone fibres that look like sparkly diamonds and that suck in the water. The wall to the left is translucent, glowing light coming through a plastic barrier so you could be looking down on the second pool at the Y, the small pool, and seeing Gus Paxton reaching his hand inside your bathing suit that time, if there was glass there.

The mystery is where does the mangy bad wet smell emanate from? What is sucking in the wetness, holding in the smell of its stuckness that none of the janitors or administrators of maintenance know how to reach?

There's another steel door, then you're going down some more zig-zaggy tiled stairs holding the railing so as not to slip and feeling quiet because you don't make stomping sounds if you're on tile stairs with concrete under them. It's muted. And it's early morning but you're late.

The new coach says to just call him Coach. What is Coach going to think of me being late?

Arriving at the pool, you know what Coach doesn't know, that thirty feet away is the other door, the door that leads to outside for the times it's so bad that Sally used to open it to help stop the asphyxiation from chlorine, the new air from outside combined with truck exhaust from the truck delivering bread for the Y cafeteria, mixing in, causing condensation to create above the pool and form a spooky, funny fog in the far shallow end, so you don't want to swim lengths anymore, you want to stand up and make your hands into Halloween tree claws and be the spooky grasping thing in the fog.

Coach doesn't know either it's the same door that leads to the bottom of the stairwell from the picture in the newspaper showing where Selena was dead.

LEAVES

Yvonne Nowak and I decide that what Coach would like is maple leaves to represent being in Canada to send back to his family and friends in Australia. We're picking a lot because it's very hard to choose the most beautiful. Coach lives across from the public library on Queen Street, in a red brick building with wooden stairs you walk up on the back, kitty-corner to the Y.

Coach is old but he has a young wife with dark hair and eyes. She used to be a swimmer but not a very good one because I've never heard of her. It seems strange that someone from Australia would have dark colouring. She's glamorous, hair swept up, dangly shiny earrings, but she has a desperate look in her eyes. It's not obvious though; it's way at the back, like she was tricked. She has two toddlers with proper blond Australian hair, so they must have got their hair colour from him.

Whenever she sees you she doesn't recognize you. It's like he has one of us for his wife. Only then we hardly ever see her.

PLANNING

What was so great about our old coach Sally was the part about setting goals. It wasn't about some freaky great achievement. It was just about trying to make a time. You set a time goal that was kind of hard for down the road, then in between smaller ones helping you get to the bigger one.

I did that and next thing I got my first trophy and next after that I was already Ontario champion in the one hundred metre freestyle with a new provincial record.

GETTING THE GUY

At the end of the swim meet it's Garth Rhodes in the lobby, Canadian champion, daddy long legs, his hair going in waves even more like mine than mine. It's Ottawa, the capital of Canada. He's seeing me waiting in the lobby resting on my grandfather's old fishing bag, which is what I'm using for my swim bag lately instead of a regular Adidas or Speedo one because I like the idea of ocean and fishing and grandfather behind it and because it makes me feel good and we're talking about it maybe because he's from British Columbia where the other ocean is, when I never expected anyone to notice, anyone like him.

Also I bet he heard about my new provincial record.

BEFORE

What happened to granny, my mom's mom: first they were thinking she was crazy and putting her away. Then at the same time granddad was riding his bike down the highway in Gaspé and got hit by a car and almost killed.

The good thing for granny, everyone says, is she never knew. She never knew about my brother because it happened after she got sick. What she got instead before was brain cancer.

NOT TALKING ABOUT IT

Two strange things about the first time seeing granny in the hospital are her hair is grey, which means she used to be dyeing it brown but it was really grey underneath. She couldn't talk.

This is an example of how Cindy and Cal are the same. Cindy was just talking to her and brushing her hair and Cal was normal too.

I'm looking at her lying halfway seated in her white-sheets hospital bed with her eyes that grey-green colour of the secrets of the ocean a certain amount out in stormy weather or an overcast day. And how her eyes show how she feels with the happiness of seeing us in them. But not knowing the meaning for certain because of what it was that got stuck in there that wouldn't let her say any more. Then I'm in the background with the life-saving machines. I'm near the door. Drifting like in water. Because of starting to feel that exact same stuck thing getting stuck inside my chest inside of me. And breathing coming harder and faster. Like gasping for air.

Because I'm not doing it anymore. Because sometimes people expect too much. I'm outside under the fresh June trees and on the sidewalk beside the pink peonies. It's sunny and squinting and I'm with dad and Uncle Stu, Aunt Sylvia's husband.

INDOOR POOL

After visiting granny, mom and Aunt Sylvia are talking, feet dangling in Aunt Sylvia's apartment's indoor pool. They're like two crows, their voices scratching and scraping at each other. But it's okay because granddad's favourite bird is the crow because of the intelligence, the ability to steal and keep shiny things.

He was mean to granny because he used to take all the money and drink all weekend and leave her with nothing but now he sits on the back stoop in Gaspé, a grin in his cheeks and eyes, watching the crows' slippery moves. Actually now he's at a different hospital taking physiotherapy for his shortened leg he was supposed to lose and his hand and his other leg.

I get a Tylenol and get to be there with them. Soon I'll go under the pool water to smooth out my headache and my red face from not stopping crying all day.

Even though I'm still on the outside of it, just looking at the patterns the light makes on the water softens the walls and mom's pleading with Aunt Sylvia to see what she's so angry about, to see their mom her way.

STARTING

For Yvonne Nowak's period starting she wouldn't bother to tell her mother about it. Her mother is too old and unaware of what is going on. Yvonne's mother isn't fat but her body goes out like a triangle from her shoulders from having no waist anymore. She wears the housecleaning-lady kind of dresses but they're so thin and old you can see how far her breasts are hanging down and to the side so there's a big space of flat chest in between them. There's no point for Yvonne telling her. It would just make everything more complicated.

She wouldn't ask her older sister who lives in an apartment in Toronto what to do because she's too far away.

When it was my period my mom started me out with pads you attach to your underwear then moved me up to tampons to push inside when I was ready. For Yvonne I'm starting her off right away with tampons because pads are so cumbersome. It's what Yvonne wants too.

We're at the movies Saturday afternoon. It's hard for Yvonne to enjoy because of how much it's hurting her. She's trying to keep it to herself so only an occasional frightened look in the dark is telling me. Maybe she didn't push it in all the way.

BOOK

Since he's Australian, Coach coaches us in the Australian style, which means swimming more lengths than ever. A lot of times we do over eight thousand metres each workout and we work out two times a day.

After a while you get used to it. Looking at the numbers added up on the blackboard at the end of the practice could be like the greedy feeling of winning a jar full of jelly beans all for yourself for guessing the right number in it, which I once did.

It was at Sonya Koba's birthday party. But then Sonya's mom gave me a dirty look because I wasn't sharing and she said I should be because I had braces on my teeth so I shouldn't be eating the jelly beans in the first place anyway.

Coach is writing a book about us, about how his coaching techniques are turning us into stars, for posterity.

Coach tells us to start our next sets when the green hand on the pace clock reaches the number. It's interesting because Australia's colour is green and ours is red and all our old coaches used to make us go on the red.

IMPORTANT

With Coach you feel like he's doing this magical thing to you, except you're doing it yourself by swimming the lengths; that's going to sweep you up into a swirl of accomplishment.

But he ignores that you don't want to be swirled. If you're at a swim meet he gives you this special kind of sugar candy that he says is good but you don't know what's in it, just take it, and then before your race he rubs your back but he rubs it too low towards the bottom, in the sensitive part around your hips, that makes you think about how he got his young wife with the blond toddlers who doesn't want to look at you.

It's not like you're exactly fighting with him, it's just eventually you realize you're not going along with him anymore. It's not like he's a bad person. It's just like a quiet frustrated knowing of each other, and knowing that he doesn't care.

MOST TALENTED

Since I'm the only one who qualifies for nationals (you have to make some very fast times) I'm like Coach's all of your eggs in one basket. It's a gloomy feeling being alone with him, just us, with my parents watching from the stands. The environment is matching because the arena we're swimming in is all wood. There's too much dark wood. It's overwhelming with darkness.

What's nice is how the red and white buoys between the swim lanes keep the water so still and separate. And how the bright pinky-red flags for timing backstroke turns stand out like cardinals in a winter wood. I like diving into the clean and quiet pool for my events, looking through my goggles at the deep pool floor.

FLORIDA

I also make a provincial team that gets to go to Florida. When you get there you billet with families. The first family has a trampoline in their backyard. Everyone surrounds it putting their hands up when you're jumping, to catch you if you're accidentally falling off. Houses in Florida don't have basements so they have more rooms in them to make up for the missing space of basement.

The second billet's mom's idea is to take her daughter in her uniform back to her private school when the swim meet is over. It's a weird swim meet because it's during a weekday. I wonder what I'm supposed to do. They're richer than the first billets with a big fenced gate you enter and then cruise along a driveway going through an orange grove. "Can't we go to the beach?" is my idea. Her mom is angry I asked for something different from what she wants but to demonstrate politeness to a rude person we do it. Because her mom's mad, so's the daughter and she may as well bring one of her real friends too so pays no attention to me or just the attention of a person who is very much superior.

It's my only day to get a sun tan to show I went to Florida when I get back to school.

The waves say hush and reach out to try to pull you under.

CHANNEL

When you're in Gaspé you walk across the highway to the bottom part of the property that you walk through to get down to the beach. It's a bay so the water is calm.

One time when the tide is out Aunt Sylvia and I keep walking and walking and the water keeps shallow right around our knees unless it's a sandbar and then it's even lower than our knees. We are so far out.

You're stepping through stringy seaweed with rounded ends like oak leaves that you can squeeze and pull at but are rubbery and always go back to their same shape. Eventually mom is screaming at us except we don't hear because we're too far out but Aunt Sylvia notices her anyway, the hands waving even though we're facing the other shore, for us to come back.

It's because of the channel. There's a channel in the middle for the ships they made that mom says has the power to pull you down inside it.

DOGS

I never realized mom's afraid of dogs. It's not because of the Bouviers from the valley killing the rabbits either. She's always been that way. I just didn't ever notice because my feelings about animals were stronger.

Or maybe she is worse.

We're coming home from going on a walk and there's a stray dog, a big one. Her being afraid works like how a blush comes over you but not starting at the head—starting from the base of your spine. It's also like a cold spray, like skunk spray, coming off of her. You can tell she wants to control and stop it but can't. The problem with it is now that it's out the dog feels it too.

It's catching. I can feel it coming up from underneath me like I'm wearing a long skirt and the wind found its way under to push it up.

Maybe it's good the dog should feel my mom's fear and now it's mine. Maybe that's the way it works. Her fear isn't telling him that it's his chance to be in command. It's telling him to watch out because she might do something crazy.

REPRESENTING

For a while I'm acting all serious at the series of swim meets in Florida to do good times and represent Ontario. I have a new bathing suit by Arena called a paper suit. It's navy blue. You wear it for races only, not for practice. It's difficult to put on because it's made so small so that when it's on it's going to be super tight making you streamlined to go faster once you get racing.

Coach got it for me. It's hard to pull it over your skin because your skin is already wet from warming up in your regular bathing suit even if you think you did a really good job drying yourself off with your towel. Then you can't tug at it too hard to compensate because the material is so thin. The material could rip. It makes you feel fat too because the tightness makes the soft flesh on your stomach seriously bulge over how far you've pulled it up already. Same when it gets to your breasts. It's such an ordeal it feels like Coach is right there with you in the girls' locker room, looking around at the other girls maybe thinking how he wishes he would have got one of them instead of you to train, forcing and helping push and prod to get you to the right way it's his idea you need to be.

It's hard to feel serious in Florida because the deck is empty. No one's in the stands cheering. It's lonely. It's sunny like no one ever heard of clouds and just a few kids that aren't even hard to beat.

SWIM TIP #3—LUCK

One of the main things for luck at swim meets is, if you're doing well, always use the same toilet. Generally swimming facilities have large washroom areas with several toilets in a row. Don't switch things up to keep it interesting. Stick with the one you started with.

If you're not doing well, switch. Usually this doesn't work. Usually once things start off wrong they don't change. But it's worth trying.

Don't lose your lucky new bathing suit Coach got you that you do good times in even though you hate putting it on.

OLYMPIC TRIALS

Olympic trials is just as difficult to get to as nationals. It's the same hard qualifying times. The difference between it and nationals is it's a separate event to select who gets to go to the Olympics.

Fortunately for Olympic trials it's not just me who qualifies and the pool's not all dark and dingy either. So that when they do the big newspaper spread on who's going it's not just me either but mainly me and Yvonne because we've made the times. They're also talking about Hanley Bell, Travis Bauman, Samantha Frye, Thelma Hyatt and Jennifer Doyle, who if they try really hard and keep improving like they are, might make the times and be able to try out.

In the newspaper picture Yvonne and I are jumping out of the water with big splash dots getting sucked up from below from our jumping as if we're beluga whales and that's what we do all day, just jump up out of the water eating the fish out of our trainers' hands for entertainment value, when really we never do that. We don't swim in a row altogether on our backs kicking and smiling up at the camera either like the way they have the others posed in their picture.

I don't see why they have to make such a big deal out of the Olympic trials when it's not like any of us have a chance of making the Olympics. I'm not saying this because I'm completely inexperienced and never had my picture in the paper before for swimming.

I'm really tired of thinking thoughts about my brother and what he did and knowing I should have already been over it. But isn't putting my picture in the paper making a big deal about how I'm representing the Y, and maybe going to make the Olympics, going to be reminding everybody?

I wonder what Selena's family is thinking when they see that picture. Aren't they wondering why I should still be getting to do so good?

ADMIRED

What I'm doing to help me keep swimming the lengths is pretending that Jeff Bevan is watching from the stands. He only watches me when we're at Wolseley Barracks for evening practice. I don't know why he only shows up there. Maybe he's like me and he doesn't like the facilities at the Y. Maybe I'm more tired at the end of the day and it's harder to keep him away.

He's from math class. He's the younger brother in my grade of the best female athlete at Central, Talia Bevan, who plays all the team sports at school, and so does he. His being there helps inspire me to go on. Sometimes he feels sorry for me but not too sorry, since he must have such a good attitude he's not going to support slacking off. Even if I do slack off sometimes, it's still pretty impressive what I do. With him I pretend to be someone who did something admirable. I wish I was.

9

LIME GREEN

Coach is leaving us. He's taking his wife and his toddlers and he's going to Alberta to a town that has the proper kind of facilities, meaning an indoor fifty-metre long-course pool, which London doesn't have, for a real swim team not like this place and this team.

Before he leaves we try the idea of me training in Tilsonburg with my old coach Sally Healy since we don't like him anymore. With that, first you get driven to Sally's house. Then you get driven to the next town over, Tilsonburg, by Sally. Then you swim around with some not very good kids you don't know including one who was one of the older guys at the London Y before Coach came and they all quit because they were too old to get used to swimming that hard all the time. Then Sally drives you back to her place and you get picked up to go where you're supposed to go next.

Sally's car is a lime-green Pacer, a weird spaceship-looking car I thought was so cool when she first got it when she was my coach before. But that's not it. It's the smell of how far her skin lotion dissolves into her skin. It's the soft blond hairs around her mouth. It's the driving beside her in the early morning quiet of her softly playing country-western radio station and the swimming round in circles right beside her on the deck and the driving home beside her too. And the assuming.

NICE POOL INTERLUDE

Tilsonburg has a nice pool, so one time the London Y held one of its swim meets there. This was when Angela White was better than me and hadn't quit swimming yet so she's in all the pictures getting the all-around champion trophy.

My dad was responsible for getting the medals to award to the winners of the events. Only instead of ribbons or regular fake metal medals, he got plastic medals. I don't know why he did that.

Then all the kids at the swim meet were laughing and, instead of calling the medals medals, calling them plastics.

SUMMER PLANS

A lot of the kids are arranging to train with the new coach we're getting in the fall who's from Waterloo, in Waterloo. But we're not doing that. We're tired of impressing new coaches.

GOING ALONG

My dad always goes along with my mom, making what she wants more important but then he's really secretly mad and blaming her a lot of the time too. Then it's like his secret message to me is you're better than your mom because you're nice and don't cause me such a problem the way she does so keep being the way I need you to be and do what your mom says.

So I'm like him more because I'm not going to be a problem. That means the plan for me this summer is to be rowing. The London Rowing Club Eight, which is what it sounds like—a rowing boat for eight rowers—has lost one of its rowers and my dad arranged with them for me to fill in and it's guaranteed to not be a problem because I'm such a good swimmer.

MAGIC SIXTEEN

My dad's older brother's way of getting out of the family was to join the British Army so then when he was sixteen he died on V-Day. Then his mom wouldn't stop crying. Then my mom's brother was the same, because he went and got killed the day before his seventeenth birthday in a freak water accident when he was being leader at a scouting camp. Then my brother was sixteen too but he didn't get killed.

WHAT

Then my father joined the military too but it was later, not during the war anymore. What he hated so much was how his mother always criticized his father and wouldn't stop, going at the words like a chicken beak pecking at little stones until it finds grain. Never not hungry.

But my father was feeling mad at his father too for being all puffed up like a rooster from doing so well in business during the war, getting rich compared to everyone else, but it was only because of the war bonds and his being lucky enough to get the government contract for them. It was nothing his father did, and my dad hating the feeling of being on the same side as his mom.

Then my dad was flying in his plane and it went down in the ocean and he almost drowned, it was going all red, it was a near-death experience and I wouldn't have been born or if I was I would have been someone different, so he decided to go to New Zealand but could only get Canada.

TRAINING

The girls on the Eights crew keep winning the provincial championships. That's what we're doing. We're training to win them again. It's so expected.

Being with them is what it must be like to join an ant colony if ants were like that and allowed other ants to join and didn't just think of them as interlopers and another source of food. It's nothing personal. It's business.

Before we get to the boat on the river part we go for a ten-kilometre run. Running around Springbank Park and Storybook Gardens, past the peacocks and reindeer behind their fences, around the geese and the green geese's feces not behind fences, looking across the river to the other side, all tall green trees; I've never been over there. Wondering what it is over there.

There's something not being said about the girl whose

place I'm taking but nothing worth resenting me over. It's nice that no one questions whether I can do the job even though I've never rowed before. Still I wonder how they measure individuals on the team when they need to.

TOPSIDE

Despite the juicy cool feeling of running under huge shady trees and off a river breeze and then the part when we get in the boat and skedaddle on the water top, our eight oars the water spider's legs, the teeny shouting coxswain our small collective head, I'm craving to plunge under the river's surface, into its dreamy blur, to rip off the stale filmy cooked-on extra layer, the skin of everyday acquaintance, that stops you from going down.

I think it would be nice for them too—nice if this sleek congregation of the Eight could also get to do that.

MORE ANTS

The time my dad's sister and husband and two teenage kids came over from England to visit us my mom got so frustrated with his sister that by the time she asked for cheese sauce instead of the white sauce my mom was making, my mom added the parmesan cheese too fast, not noticing until too late that it had been infested with red ants.

So she came around and told all us kids, I mean of our family, not theirs, not to eat the cheese sauce; she just put out the sauce separate from what it was going on, to add on. I think that was her best satisfaction to know that we all knew, including my dad, there were little red bugs in the sauce and maybe even secretly wishing one of us accidentally said something about it. She was feeling that helpless about them.

SORRY MOONS

But my dad still felt sorrier for my mom because of how mean her mom was to her, like that time when my mom was a little girl and her mother was screaming down at her sitting in the chair. And was holding her by the arms and squeezing them at the same time so the white marks stayed and the nails dug in making little red crescent moons and the finale was how my mom was so bad she was as bad as her dad, she was just like her dad.

That was what was so bad about her.

RELIGION

The other thing my dad was getting away from when he left England was religion. My dad was good at not telling you anything about it, just leaving it in his past and not a problem across the ocean with his family, but it was being Roman Catholic, which was from his mom's side.

WAR

Where my dad's mom came from was the First World War. Her family was big round peasants in the field in France a day from the sea, making bread and filling it with shallots from the garden and cheese from the goats. Then using the crusts from the bread to clean out what was left at the bottom of their bowls that had been full of stew.

Then his dad, afraid from war and having skinny white rooster legs under his khaki army uniform.

REASON

Whereas with my mom's mom, the reason the doctors and everyone were saying she was mad, like crazy mad, and were going to lock her up was because she was so mad, like angry mad, for so long.

But getting brain cancer is much cuter because if you get brain cancer everyone goes, oh poor you, because instead of staying mad you did a nice thing and turned it into a little worm in your head, or maybe if you were writing you would change a letter for starting a sentence, especially the letter O, the first letter of my granny's name, into a cute little smiley face with long curly eyelashes.

And then you, the family, get to be all righteous to the doctors: "How could you say such terrible things about my granny, my goodness! How dare you suggest it could be something mental?"

Our family is so perfect. It couldn't possibly be!

COOKIE JAR

Visiting granny and granddad in Montreal there would always be granny's cookies in the cookie jar on the kitchen table and granny watching us taking them from her spot beside the stove with a quirky smile and her eyes glassy like she was seeing in us something funny she remembered.

Soft, with raisins in them and nuts and with white creamy

sugar icing on the top, and with allspice, the secret ingredient. There wouldn't be any point fighting over the biggest. Every one of them was the biggest.

BECAUSE

Aunt Sylvia's different from my mom because she grew tall. Her skin is regular. It's not all freckled. She has long black hair compared to my mom's called red, but really shiny orange like new pennies.

Don't you think it's possible what Aunt Sylvia was saying to my mom was true, that granny wasn't that bad to her? Mom won't even talk to her anymore. Even if Aunt Sylvia was wrong shouldn't she be entitled to her own opinion about her own mother? Maybe for her it wasn't the same anymore.

Then for us it was mainly just granny's cookies.

KILLER INSTINCT

Dad says to me, in that joking way he does because he tries to avoid hurting your feelings but sometimes he likes to say what he thinks too, that I don't have the killer instinct. Not having it is why I don't perform better than I do at swimming.

Why would he say something like that to me? Did he choose those words on purpose or do you think he said them the way people do as a manner of speech? And not thinking of how close to who you think you are the words might be?

Does dad really want me to have the killer instinct, to be like what Cal did? Would that be better?

NEITHER HERE

I also don't agree with him saying about it being good and granny never knowing about Cal. Just because she was dying and couldn't talk doesn't mean she couldn't tell something wasn't right from how we were acting and what it was we weren't saying anymore.

What other purpose did she have in that hospital bed for her brain-cancer-riddled brain she got in a bad marriage, had kids and never got to go to college with? Wouldn't the helpless impersonal grief of your own stupid wordless dying make the reason for the pain she felt in the place Cal was missing more obvious? Sometimes I feel sorry for my dad the way he thinks he has to keep things hidden to keep giving the good impression he thinks other people need him to give.

FOURS

For rowing this summer besides the Eights, I'm also on a Fours team made up of all new rowers. One is Samantha Fry from the swim team who also decided to come along with me rowing for the summer instead of swimming. Fours don't have a coxswain. So I'm chosen the leader, the one at the front of the boat whose job it is to set the stroke pace.

Maybe what's better about me than the other three girls the rowing coaches can measure is my swimming reputation.

Another is Ingrid Fischer who is originally from Sweden. Ingrid is telling us how everyone in Sweden takes their clothes off to take saunas together and doesn't even think about it, meaning sex. Then they get naked in the middle of the winter and go into the freezing cold ocean too, also never thinking about it. (Sex.)

The Fours get third in provincials, a bronze medal—pretty good for novices. In the Eights we get first like we're supposed to.

OVERARCHING

There used to be pictures of dad in the paper, regular, small, showing his existence to go along with the story of his leadership in the union or his party the New Democratic Party, the political group about everybody sharing and being fair that nobody votes for. Mouth open like a fish, saying something important and political to match the story in the article and his intent indignant brow. His big black-frame glasses on his face.

10

NEW COACH

Our new coach, Sean Bradley, is actually handsome but in a punched-in kind of way. There's no punch marks really. I think it's the small cheekbones with the colour of the bags under his eyes combining. Also he holds his full lips in this pursed way and never just lets his chin be—he's always holding in his chin muscles. Then he has these really nice laughing, smiling eyes in the middle of it but everything else around them is telling you you're not welcome to come in.

So he's going to start us off by jogging down to the river

and around a section of it for the first week instead of going straight to the swimming pool.

It's like he has a chip on his shoulder and if it comes to comparing chips you're going to let his chip win.

I jog with Yvonne and on the way back to the Y we stop in on my mom's bookstore since I'm bored of having been jogging all summer for rowing and it's not going to matter anyway. We get special drinks and instead of it being an author or her friend Lana or another friend come to visit sitting in the smoky backroom, it's us—we're the guests of honour.

Outside the trees are beginning to lose their leaves for fall, the sky darkening coming on earlier. City and winter getting ready to join together to fold me up inside like what goes in a sandwich.

ENGLISH CLASS

Mr. Voight is always referring to things my last year's English teacher, Mr. McDermott, said. The reason he must constantly refer to Mr. McDermott is because he's so insecure in his own knowledge. He can't even tell for a while how I'm smart.

Just when he finally starts to notice (maybe Mr. McDermott told him) he gives the class an assignment in which you're supposed to describe how witnessing an atom bomb explosion would make you feel. He loves mine, he says. But it needs to be written more coherently. Like with regular sentences.

I know how to write in regular sentences. Evidently it is Mr. Voight's belief that when you witness a nuclear bomb blowing up, no matter how upsetting you might be finding it, your experience should be described paying full attention to the proper rules of grammar. So he's giving me this example of the kind of thing he wants, which is a photocopy of another kid's work from the other grade ten class he teaches and I guess it's okay.

Actually it's not. There may even have been a rainbow in it. It's making me even more upset because the girl, I recognize her handwriting, has this perfect curly-cue script that is just so prissy and perfect, which for some reason is even more evident in its smudgy photocopied form. Which I know the handwriting isn't really part of it or fair to judge. How could he love her work and mine the way he says he does?

I'm trying to do what he says making it like hers but keeping the essence of mine. I'm trying. But I can't tell anymore. And when he's giving it back to me, not mean or blaming really, just disappointed in an amazed way along the lines of what happened to it and how I ruined it.

DOMINANCE

Usually what happens is some of the younger kids start coming up, start getting good, keeping up with you in practice and then it's like you have to fend them off, to maintain your dominance. You're still friends, if you like them that is. But at the same time you have to keep them down.

One area I've always maintained my dominance is the Public Utilities Commission city finals. At this point, it's not a very serious swim meet but since I was ten no one's beat me for the overall city championship. Even when Angela White was getting way ahead of me, winning medals at the big swim meets and already making qualifying times for nationals, she still couldn't beat me for the overall city champion.

INTERMINABLY

For the swim party the McNeils have in their basement it's Ted Wilkins' idea, a normal guy who normally swims two lanes down from me, to dance with me for "Hey Jude," which I don't have a problem with. I'm fine with it.

The problem is with "Hey Jude" because if you've ever danced to it you will have noticed "Hey Jude" is a song that may never end. And the fact of its going on so long is bolstering Ted's confidence in the belief his job is to force me to dance the way he wants me to. He's pressing his arms hard against mine to get me to. When regularly we're just talking about the times we did last swim meet or how hard the workout we're in is. Why is it when I'm the one having all these incomprehensible expectations being put on me, he's the one getting angrier the further along the song goes?

TYPING

This year I have typing for home room. Some of the kids are getting really good at typing already but I'm not going to be because, first of all, it's not even an academic subject. Also the teacher already likes me. She knows me already because of my mom's bookstore and she doesn't care and it doesn't prove anything about my not being smart. We know I am if I want to be and it just so happens I don't in this case.

Today my plan is to go to typing since it's home room for first period, so I'm signed in, then skip English class second period, because I have a test for history in third period that I need to study for.

The last time I came to school late when I had a dentist appointment I just told them at the office about the dentist appointment and they let me in fine, no questions asked. So I thought it'd work okay again this time even though in this case it isn't true, because of how it wasn't a problem last time.

The worst is the receptionist looking you in the eye and calling the dentist's receptionist to check if it's true and you looking her back in the eye and wondering if there's any particular point at which you might as well bail but feeling compelled to see it through, to see what the receptionist at the school looks like, precisely how she's going to raise her brow or click her tongue or perhaps even how she's going to compose her "professional, non-judgmental" face, when the receptionist at the dentist office tells her you weren't there today.

INSTEAD

The weird thing is when the principal calls my mom to tell her what I did; she gives it back to him. How there must have been a good reason. Then when she learns more from my story, what a travesty it is we students aren't given sufficient time to study for our tests.

RED BIKE

It's like the time my mom sent me on her old bike with the wicker basket, before I had my own but was tall enough to reach the pedals, to buy some bread from the A&P grocery store, which was halfway down Kipps Lane. On the way home older boys from Cal's grade made me stop and were shaking the basket so the money from the leftover change from the bread was falling on the ground.

The leader was big with thick black hair. It's because the outlines of people jiggle when they're scaring you it's hard to tell them apart from each other after when your mom is asking you who it was. It's because boys three grades up with black hair look the same as each other I said it was Neil Edmunds' big brother and my mom went right down there to his house and was getting so mad at his mom for being the kind of mom who was letting her son do that and I didn't know how to get her to stop. Even though the mom kept asking him, and he kept saying no and so she kept saying no, it wasn't him. My mom was persisting because that's how loud and brave she would always be for me, which is what I could count on her for.

Then Neil Edmunds was telling me for years it wasn't his brother and I was saying yes it was. After all that, it had to be. He was never mad at me and still liked me. Until I realized he must be right but I still didn't know who it was who did it.

UNIVERSITY GUYS

Since my new coach, Sean Bradley, is still associated with the Waterloo clubs where he used to coach not just the age-group team but also the university team, a few of the guys from the university team are coming down and training with us in London in the spring when university gets out.

First there are two. There's Roy Sutherland, a very good breaststroker, who would like to make the national team, and there's Curt Kohl, who's highly competitive all-around but it's still not clear in which area he's likely to excel, unlike his older brother, who isn't training with us, who it is clear for because he has already. Curt's older brother has exceedingly excelled. He used to be on the Canadian team.

Initially I was prepared to love both of them. With Roy, though, it wouldn't stay attached. Like he was a cat with his tail up high, rubbing his scent from his whiskers and always walking away, but I wouldn't care. But not like the way a cat is—acting like not caring, but caring. I really wouldn't care.

Whereas with Curt, there's his walk, which is quiet and relaxed like he's at home in his slippers when in reality he's on the pool deck. But the soft way of walking could also be the kind of a stealthy approach an Indian brave uses to sneak up upon the unsuspecting deer he's hunting.

There's how his waist is a little wider than it should be. There's his skin. There's the way the blood vessels, exaggerated from chlorine, have the room to look like tangled red tree roots because there's so much space to fill inside the whites of his big green cool observing, but soft like velvet, eyes.

Sometimes Curt arrives at practice late, which means I can miss him and want him and long for him. When he arrives all those feelings get answered in a single gut clenching.

NATIONALS

My first nationals with Sean I make the finals, which means the top eight in Canada, in the two hundred metre backstroke, and the consolation finals, the top sixteen, in the one hundred metre backstroke. Wow. Suddenly I'm so good! If I'm already this good without even thinking about it I'm wondering how much better I can get if I am thinking about it.

I wonder what Sean thinks.

A guy from Edmonton with the yellow hair that's dark black underneath, what a lot of swimmers get from the chlorine, and green mucus hanging from his nose is smiling up at me that time in the warm-up pool before I go in to start mine. But you know that can happen to anyone, especially in pools—the mucus.

And then, in the Holiday Inn, hotel room doors open, partying before we come home that's him lying on top of me pushing his tongue in my mouth and me letting him. And Curt coming by right then like maybe I secretly wanted him to so I could look up at him entreatingly with the wish of how do I get this guy off of me and make you be the one who likes me and Curt not doing anything besides seeing, walking past the door, quietly, like in slippers.

HOW THINGS WORK MOON

The moon is always showing the same side of itself to earth. It times its rotation that way. If the moon was human it would be acting like someone hiding having a big ugly mole on the back of their body. Or if they were in a science-fiction story an extra limb. Everyone calls the other side of the moon the dark side.

Sometimes the moon might be feeling like its dark side is getting larger and taking over. When the moon is waning it looks that way. Like a tennis ball went over the fence and landed in a swimming pool and it was the fall so no one was paying attention to fish it out. And the tennis ball was getting more water-logged, losing its buoyancy, the round floating part of itself sticking out of the water growing less and getting dragged under.

Like whenever I'm swimming by the deep end at the big pool at the downtown Y and seeing the drain hole at the bottom of the pool every time I am imagining swimming down and not being able to stop myself exploring its metal openings with my fingers and my fingers getting stuck in it and staying submerged and no one noticing and never coming back up.

But it's wrong what people say about the dark side of the moon. It's not dark. It gets the same amount of sunlight as our side, the side facing earth. People just think that because they can't see it, it's dark.

PIANO

The summer is long-course season, which I'm better at. Long course is a fifty-metre pool. Short course is twenty-five. I have what is called a long stroke, which suits a longer pool better. In a fifty-metre pool I'm like how a racing car is described, I get a chance to open it up and put it into overdrive, but in a short-course pool you get to the end of the length and have to turn and everything is disrupted before you get that chance.

Since the only long-course pool in London is an outdoor pool that is only open two months a year, we're going to start training long course in Waterloo on the weekends a few months before when we regularly start.

The reason it's a good idea is that it takes a while to get used to the long-course pool. If you don't build up your conditioning for long course what's going to happen to you when you're racing is you're going to "die."

Dying goes like this. You're on the last length of your race. You're only five or ten or fifteen metres from the wall to the finish. Your limbs get so heavy, it's like they're made of iron or anything else that sinks. You can barely move, especially your arms. Moments ago it looked like you were poised to win the race. Now you're so weak, your arms look pathetic like spaghetti, you're probably going to finish dead last.

It's also called "when the piano drops."

FAN

I have a fan. It's another kid's dad from a different city. He saw me win my first provincial long-course medal, which was the first time he came up to me. He has an orange handlebar moustache. His eyes are so pale they're almost not there. The way of how he asks me questions is like his acknowledgement of how I am a beautiful swimmer and because of it there's something special about me. It's nice.

When someone is so nice to you everything around you opens up so you can notice it's all there for a change. The kid's dad is behind a fence. It's the fence around the pool. I see trees in the distance.

PRACTICE SWIMMERS

There's a kind of swimmer that coaches never get mad at. No one blames them. These swimmers train so hard in practice. They are exemplary trainers. But when it comes to a swim meet it's like they have nothing left.

Sometimes it takes a while to figure out who they are. Like Debbie Healy whose mom Sally was our coach before. Debbie went all the way to Thunder Bay to train with Frank Jones, the most productive coach in Canada, who was turning Canadian swimmers into "achieving machines" in the Thunder Bay team colour of winning baby-blue bathing suits and who loved her because she trained so hard, which my mom said I could too if I wanted, go to train under him in Thunder Bay. Frank Jones would never say a bad word about Debbie. Still something about her wouldn't rise to the top like cream.

BLOOD

Another time Debbie Healy was still one of the bigger kids and still training with us at the Bob Hayward Y and had to run to the locker room because the blood was all gushing down her leg. Then when I just started getting my period, my mom said, "Don't worry about it when you're swimming, the swimming stops it. You never saw Debbie Healy with any problem, did you?" She used Debbie because Debbie was so worthy of being looked up to so of course she could never have a problem during a swim practice, which is exactly what I did see so how could I tell her that? It would be like a slap in the face it would be so exactly contradictory. Couldn't she have said anyone else? Because it only ever happened to Debbie that I saw. Then maybe I could bring up the incident of Debbie as how I just so happened to see it happen to someone else.

SPECIAL

One of the girls from the regular Waterloo swim club is training with us too because Sean allowed her because of her strong training ethic. She is two years younger than me and keeping up with Curt Kohl with the distance trainers. (Curt started working on trying to specialize in the distance events.) She's keeping up with guys more than five years older than her!

Then she's crying for three swim meets in a row because she turns out to be one, a practice swimmer, and then she's not training with us anymore. She must be smart because why keep swimming so hard like that when your body doesn't know how to stand out when it counts?

Sometimes I think half of the guys on our team are that way. With Hanley Bell maybe it's when the coach came in from Australia to train us, he burned him out. Hanley doesn't sit beside the poolside like Travis Bauman, ripping bits off the top of the Styrofoam cup his mom put water in and froze in the freezer the night before until the ice part sticks out far enough so he can rub round red marks on his shoulder with his feet dangling in the water. Then maybe the next week it's the other shoulder that's hurting so he's still not able to join us practicing our thirty by one hundred metre repeats, the first ten sets starting at a one minute and forty second pace time and descending from there. Which is a very hard set.

Like he pushed Hanley to make him good before his time. It's like he didn't care about what was inside of him to come out when it was ready. It's like he raped him.

Now every time Hanley races up and down the pool he's got this mad look on his face, like "Why can't I do it?", like a "I will do it, despite you all!" face. And he makes his arms go forceful and hard like he's almost found his passion.

DRIVE

I wonder if Curt Kohl might be like that too. That he can't figure out what it is about his older brother that makes him such a good swimmer but if he just sticks around long enough he'll catch it.

He might be laughable. Cassie Fowler is laughing at him. She's telling me that Curt keeps staring at her like he has a crush on her. I saw it. I saw him looking at her that way. At the wall, before he pushed off for his next repeat.

But I think he's just doing it to her because of me, because of being able to tell how I feel, like a way of showing how he would look and act if I was able to permit him to care. Cassie doesn't care. She could if she wanted.

In a way, I think everybody loves him, not just me, because of the way he keeps staying swimming like he loves swimming. So you have to keep taking him seriously even though he's not improving in swim meets. What's different about him: his eyes aren't the small, figuring out what's expected of them, go-along kind as everybody else. They're just in the place where they are. Even if it's wrong or not very smart, you have to let it be. You have to respect it.

SUSPECT

Mr. Voight, my English teacher, wants to talk to me outside of class because of being flippant. I say, "What is flippant?" Even though I know, because how could you not know what that word means, it sounds exactly like what it is, only really I'm not a hundred per cent certain and with his intelligence so suspect there's nothing to lose. Could it be possible Mr. Voight is using a word he doesn't even know the meaning of?

Bad call—the reason he knows I find out is because three weeks later it's in our class's "Words Are Important" vocabulary lesson.

SPEECHES

For our improvised speeches unit my plan is to do mine like this kid in our class, Patrick Logan. Patrick can take any subject and make something up out of it off the cuff, completely hilarious. It looks so easy.

For picking your speech subject you pick one of two choices then you go out in the hallway for a few minutes to come up with what you're going to say. It's a hallway in the new section of the school that has the new kind of coloured plastic lockers lining it. They're a nice bold blue. I know nothing about the topic I picked. The lights are brighter in this new hallway section of the school than anywhere else. I have no clue how to be smart or funny the way Patrick Logan is.

When Mr. Voight opens the door to the class for my turn I tell him I'm going to do the other topic I drew after all, the one about your hobby. Mr. Voight cooperates, not noticing any rule-bending. My hobby is swimming. I sound great when I talk about swimming. I'm insouciant, meaning (Mr. Voight isn't the only one going to benefit from "Words Are Important") casual, about the experience of the winning and the different places I've been. There's the empty listening sound of a little bit of awe in the classroom. There's funny parts. I'm funny.

11

BILLETS

Hanley Bell and I drive down to Waterloo together in his pickup truck on Friday nights and go to our separate billets.

First Sean set me up with this fat girl three years younger than me smiling like I was going to be her role model. I was imagining a too soft bed with a flowery bedspread and one of those bedside lamps with the elaborate swishy shades and her parents always smiling at me like I was a fairy princess and with her admiring me but with the fact of her gunning to beat me always having to be there too.

When Sean heard I didn't like that idea he switched me to the Millers'. He just did it without even telling me he was going to until he did. I never would have expected him to make a change like that about what I felt to make me happy. The Millers' has a younger sister who doesn't swim and a tall, sticklike university brother who is only training with us in Waterloo and not coming back to London during the week. It also has another older brother attached to it. He doesn't live at home anymore or swim but is the star of all because he is the one fierce and smart enough to have figured out how to get on the Olympic team. He got on in this sneak attack kind of way, under the radar, no one seeing it coming except the people close to him, like Sean, and even them amazed at his ability to pull it off against the odds, proving even more the power of his will and of his strategic intelligence.

DOLLARS FOR DOUGHNUTS

My parents give me five dollars or ten dollars to give to Hanley for gas depending but his parents are already giving him money for gas too. So after a few weekends I tell him I'll just keep the money. Hanley doesn't need it.

That way when we stop at Tim Horton's for doughnuts on Sunday night on the way out of town, I've got plenty of money, easily enough for two doughnuts, two crullers—one chocolate walnut, one with cherries. For eating them, first I take care of the doughy insides, practically a chore, then I finish off with the best part, the crispy sugary crust. But I eat them in a way that is careful not to make a mess of Hanley's truck.

Eating two doughnuts sounds bad but it actually fits with

my strategic plan, which is to eat hardly anything all during the weekend when I'm training in Waterloo, so not only will I be a great athlete, I'll be a slim and beautiful one too.

SWIM TIP #4—SOGGY TOWELS

There's two options for towels during the week.

Since practice is at one pool in the morning and another at night and you don't go home in between, you have the choice of taking one towel for both practices or two towels, one for each.

Two towels, one for each practice is too hard. There's not enough room for two towels in your knapsack. It's too bulky with all your school stuff in there too.

With one towel, you use it to dry yourself off after morning swim practice. You stuff it with your bathing suit wrapped inside of it in your knapsack at the bottom of your locker at school. (Never consider keeping your bathing suit in a separate bag to prevent its wetness from further dampening the towel. This would put you in the position of having to put on practically a completely soaking wet cold bathing suit for second practice. Do not do it.) Before second practice pull out the damp towel in preparation for drying yourself off after practice. What helps is exposing it to air at practice for the two hours up high, away from wet, on a hook on the wall by the pool deck. But the towel is still damp when you're done. It doesn't help much.

STEAK OF OLYMPIANS

Towards the end of staying at the Millers' the parents go out of town for the weekend and the big brother, the Olympian, Steve, even though he doesn't live there, hosts a party that includes a barbeque with juicy red steak meat he's bought special. He's mad at me because I don't want the steak. He's red-hot mad like steak-cooking briquettes when you blow on them.

It's my first time meeting Steve. I wonder if my staying sleeping in the Millers' cold dark basement in the room beside the TV room where we stay up late—with other guys from the team including Curt Kohl coming over sometimes too—and watch Saturday Night Live makes him think I'm in his family now, makes him think it's important I should eat my meat.

Or maybe this is a secret ceremonial rite of passage for getting to the Olympics, the thing you have to do first, and he knows I'm "the one" out of all of us training in Waterloo on the weekend. Maybe it's why Sean decided I should billet here after all, because as a future Olympian I'm supposed to take up the gauntlet and eat the steak.

MULTIPLES OF FOUR

Not the last Olympics but the one before the last Olympics, mom rented a special TV, colour and much bigger than ours, so we could watch everything. Since then I put all regular birthday wishes on hold for making the Olympics. I found out what I was supposed to be wishing for.

Watching TV during the day, even colour TV, the light of the day gets on the screen turning it grey and like you're in the past. Dust dots move in slow motion in the sun rays. The clean window to outside glares and hurts your eyes.

A lot of German girl swimmers with pale skin and underarm

hair under big man shoulders were standing on the podium in their Arena brand bathing suits. Winning.

They were having their way just like my mom always does.

THE ROAD

Hanley says my mom should expand her store into several locations like his dad's is. "That's the fun of it," he says.

"Oh really," I say back, not interested but not showing it. Surprised he supposedly is.

With Hanley—he's the only boy of four kids in his family—the idea is that when he grows up he will take over the family jewellery business because of being the boy.

What's similar about us is the family pressure we feel on our heads.

One of the reasons why Hanley has to walk around being all sober and responsible-looking all the time is because of the pressure of all of those sisters on his being the privileged one picked out to take over.

EXAGGERATED

Except for Hanley, his whole family is exaggerated-looking. A lot of it has to do with the breasts. His mother always wears dresses when most of the other moms wear pants and the dresses have the big round low-cut front. While her breasts are really big and they really stick out, they're also a little bit placid-looking because the line between them is perfectly straight and it goes benignly on and on like you're never going to get to the end of them.

Hanley's mom is high-coloured as well; her complexion can get very red, which doesn't just show on her face but on her bosom too. To get the entire picture remember, because of the jewellery store, she's always wearing a fancy necklace and matching earrings.

The second sister, the one right before Hanley, has the same look as her mom, with dark hair too and a sweet co-operative face. Her breasts are way springier though. You can't imagine how she's going to keep them in her bathing suit like any second one might spring out and pop you in the face. Or maybe they're like magnetic tractor beams and if you don't watch it your face will get sucked into her bosom.

The worst is the sister after him who's a year younger than me in age-group swimming because her face is more mean-looking, like her dad, and when she's in the locker room changing you can see they grew too fast and are all reddish-purple stretch marks. What she also likes to do is make deep belching sounds and follow through on the belch by leaving her mouth wide open and contorted.

SPACE

After Hanley's family moved to a new house just outside of town because of how well his dad's business is doing, he invited the swim team over. From the front the house just looks like a regular ranch-style but in the back you can see it's built into a hill and there's this whole other floor facing out for the sunsets and a big deck. It's a big house.

I was glad to see Hanley had a lot of room to himself around all of those sisters of his.

About his oldest sister, under her clothes her breasts look normal. She doesn't swim anymore. But she might even feel the most oppressive to Hanley because she's so involved in the business already, like she's the one it really belongs to, not him. Hanley is still only in high school.

ATTITUDE

Hanley's attitude to swimming is—if only this could mean as much to me as what taking over my father's business is supposed to mean to me.

FISHING

The last time we went to Gaspé we went out on a fishing boat with some of my mom's and our cousins. We were leaving the mouth of the Gaspé harbour, heading out to open ocean and then along to Percé Rock, watching on the radar screen image below deck the schools of fish looking black and white and fuzzy like Eskimo etchings on soapstone.

Cindy kept staying under the deck getting seasick in the stuffy cabin not listening to the trick I discovered to not get seasick of staying up on top of the deck in the wet and spray even if it was raining a little.

Mom was pointing at the whales, elated and instructive of never to forget, seeing the whales pressing up and surfacing so parts of them came out over the water like the way dolphins do only bigger than dolphins but not the really big kind of whales.

CINCINNATI

After all that long-course training, by the time we get to Cincinnati in the middle of the summer, I win every single event Sean puts me in and make the national qualifying times in each as well. I'm magnificent. I'm the star. I get the all-around trophy.

Curt Kohl does medium the same as he usually does.

At swim meets I'm waiting on moments to be in the same vehicle, the same room. Our eyes touch, mine pretending not to be big gaping holes. In the pool our voices can be together above water in the middle of the air. Like two bubbles floating up happening to coincide.

I would be happy just going on like that with him in water. Or maybe if I got a lot more first-place finishes he would say something more to me, notice me the way I want. He couldn't refuse. If I could, by a kind of loving force of will, get him to do it, to see me, to want me, I'd be free. I wouldn't be doing anything wrong. Being someone who could never be trusted because of who they might be inside when not kept under control wouldn't matter anymore. How many more lengths would it take?

Sometimes in practice it gets so strong it's like being pushed along an ocean current, and when I measure my heart with my finger on my throat to get the count so Sean can know how good my conditioning is, it's barely beating any faster it's becoming so normal.

PROBLEM CAT MOON

If you're the moon being visited by human spaceships you don't get to say what it is you get. You can't control it. What you get is golf carts, flags, commemorating plaques. They take rock samples.

Like sometimes you get up in the morning, go out the front door and your cat brought you home a mouse it killed and left it on the front doorstep. It's the problem cat your mom doesn't like that eats wool she was nice enough to take in from someone getting rid of but isn't going to keep. It's not working out.

But what you should do is appreciate the gesture of the mouse. It's not like a dead mouse is what you always wanted or anything. Why can't your mom just tuck things made of wool away somewhere the cat can't get at? Why does she have to quit on everything so fast? Why is no one ever good enough?

THANK YOU

It's the last weekend before the outdoor long-course pool in London opens and we won't be going to Waterloo anymore. We're only training for one day so technically I don't even have to go to my billet's house. But I'm going over anyway, just for the afternoon in between practices, because I feel it's important to show my appreciation to the Millers for billeting me. I'm asking my mom for gift ideas. Her idea is a nice plant. It's a Piggyback plant. A Piggyback plant has a big heart-shaped leaf below with a smaller one growing out of it over top. It's in a hanging planter.

Maybe not such a smart gift idea because the plant is big and delicate and awkward to transport between cities and pool and cars. The Millers' mom takes it. Her teeth smile. She looks at me like she knows all about me from what happened during the weekend she went away. Maybe more.

She looks at me like she's glad I won't be coming back like she knows I don't care about her son, Scott, the one who followed me into the bathroom and cleaned up after me the vomit from drinking beer but not eating steak, which I would have done myself, like the way I always am, taking care of everything, which I like to, if time didn't have to get all twisted like that. And which she's right about, I don't care about Scott like that and I never acted like I did.

Which now I have to follow through on too this afternoon and be respectful of his unspoken sudden caring-for of me, the timing of which shows how unserious he is because I won't be coming back again and neither will he; he doesn't train in London.

Because I owe him for being glad about and liking me for not doing what his older brother wanted me to do, for me meaning something to him for it, like together we make a kind of mutually grateful ganging up on.

INSIDE

It's like when I leave the house to hang out with Scott on his skateboard on the street. Or maybe later when she's absolutely certain I'm gone, that Scott has taken me back to practice. She's going to pick up the Piggyback plant from where she's placed it on the kitchen counter. And, one at a time, methodically, like limb by limb, rip the pretty lacy branches right out from their roots.

Like she knows who I am and where I come from isn't right. And she should never have let me step inside her house.

12

MAKING THE TEAM

Three of us from the London Y make the provincial team to compete at the Canada Games in Newfoundland: Hanley Bell, my friend who I don't get to see that much because they keep the guys separate; Nick Casteel, a conceited breaststroker originally from Halifax who whenever you talk to him acts like it's because you can't stop yourself from trying to get closer to the power of his future greatness; and me. It's another one of those pools that's in a building with a dark wood interior, like farm animals in a barn.

But it was already starting to happen before the Canada Games.

At nationals in Montreal everybody was walking to the pool from the hotel, about a mile away, on a sidewalk between a big leftover field they didn't use making the Olympics and a busy street. But what I like to do for swim meets is get driven around, holding it all in still and quiet, until the sound of the starter's gun. Then explode.

It's not because I'm lazy. It's because being that way at swim meets is effective. What's the point of chatting and frittering it all away in the too sunny open sky? These guys, my teammates, don't even know how to make it matter. They act serious but are clowns.

Also it was the middle of summer and the air conditioning wasn't working in my hotel room, it was too hot to sleep. I don't know how my roommate was doing it. There was no air. It was all going out of control and nothing being able to be done about it.

NOTICING

I used to be the worst starter in races. It was one of those things where you don't notice it yourself. You think you're fine and everything is normal. Meanwhile everyone around you is noticing something seriously wrong about you—about your starts. I thought my swim starts were perfectly fine.

Then my dad gets Mr. Thompson, the dad of some other kids on the team who sometimes assists with coaching, over at our house. I'm practicing by diving off the deck into our above-ground swimming pool over and over. It's like I'm allowing Mr. Thompson, because my dad says I can, into my head to reach in and turn on the "how to start" switch. And now I don't remember how I used to start before. It's like I used to be one of the dumb kids but now I'm one of the smart kids. I'm almost always the best starter now.

READY

Sean got picked to be team coach for the provincial team too. It's serious because we're practicing all together at training camp in Toronto. Sean is making sure all the athletes are ready. I'm watching some of them training already through the glass window on the way to the locker room for my practice. I'm watching the reams of little water balls temporarily free, separated, from the tons of water still in the pool, by wild swimmers' arms and feet. Frenetic.

Now I'm here, I can't remember what I'm doing here.

GRASP

There's another guy who joined the London Y and trained with us this summer, from Windsor. He has brownish-red hair and freckles and eyes, which along with his head are exaggeratedly small, on top of and in relation to his big swimmer's shoulders. The Waterloo guys call him Raisin Eyes.

I thought the Waterloo guys were more civil than that. He doesn't defend against it, his eyes mute and sultry, shrivelled; his giant shoulders, pretty accessories.

Yvonne Nowak likes him. Yvonne would. She works hard in practice but won't stay in the leader position once she gets there. She fades and then you have to take it over again. How could you like a guy whose name is Raisin Eyes?

CARRIED

The people in Newfoundland are really happy about us being there. For example: a pair of policemen, in their police car on duty overseeing the opening ceremonies, are asking about the provincial pins we have for trading with the kids from other provinces. They want to trade their Newfoundland constabulary badges for our provincial pins. They want to take us home to show their wives for dinner. They do. They're crazy happy.

Then there's the mayor. She brings some of us on the team in her mayor's office and wants to know our opinions. We're discussing world events. Then one of us figures out there's easy access from the window in her office to go out on the roof and steal the Newfoundland flag of St. John's City Hall while she's talking to us. Then when he's having a problem detaching it a security guard sees him and is helping him.

RELAY

If I was doing the times I was in Cincinnati I'd be getting medals galore. Instead of swimming normally at the top of the water so my arms are able to get out in the air, free, to build up momentum, it's like I'm at the bottom of the pool. I think the only one who can see me where I am is my coach Sean.

What he does after my poor performances in personal events is put me as anchor for the four-by-fifty freestyle relay.

This is a tricky move on his part, which is perfectly

legitimate because it's a well-known fact coaches like to employ psychological strategies on their swimmers for right, altruistic reasons.

Everyone is relying on you when you're the anchor of the relay. You're last. There's no one after to make up for it if you perform poorly. Making me anchor is Sean's way of showing me he has faith in me to get over it all being in my head. Only what if it isn't? Besides which, realistically, what is he thinking? Swimming anchor on this particular relay would be difficult no matter how I was performing. Usually the anchor position is reserved for the best team member in the event, which in this event, the fifty freestyle, I'm not even close.

TELEGRAM

Shannon Williams, who lived across and down the street from me and who was better than me at everything including having a better mom, sent me a telegram, cheering me on.

It's the nicest thing anyone ever did. Now not only am I letting myself down and probably going to let down the other three girls on the four-by-fifty relay, I'm letting Shannon down too.

NAME

At least she spelled my name right. The Canada Games program got my name wrong. It can't be fixed. It's too big of a swim meet for them to change it now. The new name sounds like an old-lady name. It's ugly. It makes me feel lost too—and clingy.

So when I'm sprinting that one length of the pool, because it's long course and in long course fifty metres is only one length, and our team is out in front because it's given me a good lead, what I'm trying to be is this new better person. Not be against it just because it got an ugly name. Give it a chance. I'm trying not to be looking down at the pool bottom where my real self feels itself to be. I'm thinking about how it's got to be as easy as Sean's strategy is forcing me, a simple trick of the mind, a decision. While the girl from another province—maybe British Columbia, maybe Quebec, probably the best sprinter on her team, the way you're supposed to do for relays, unless they decided to employ a different strategy too—is rushing up beside me on a happy wave. So happy, she'd have a big shark grin on her face too if it wasn't so hard to grin while you're swimming a race.

OTHER

What I think Sean wants from me is to keep it pushed down to the bottom of the pool, and go on and never say, for example, about who it is I like and want for me. And in that way stop being a problem for everyone. Beat the girl from British Columbia.

Except I'm saying it doesn't work that way. It's not the decision Sean thinks it is. Because pushing it to the bottom of the pool doesn't give you back what you're missing to make you go faster either. It doesn't.

IMAGINATION

I wonder if Curt really does like me but is the kind who won't say when I need him to. I need him to say. I think he likes me.

If he was Cal he might not like it that I was doing better than him at swim meets all the time. It's not my fault I'm a good swimmer. He might hate me for grabbing all the attention to myself. Maybe I should have just let Cal be better than me and everything would have turned out okay and he wouldn't be in a psychiatric prison. No one would be dead.

I shouldn't have been such a good swimmer. I should have kept it hidden. I'm only imagining Curt would like me.

PRISON

Dad says Cal is an excellent baseball player now. He was talking to him. He says all the guys, the other guys in psychiatric hospital prison, want him on their team because he's turned into a power hitter.

The fences around Cal's jail are silver-coloured with little stars along the top. The stars are attached to wires attached to tilting-in extra posts on top of regular vertical fence posts. In actuality the stars are pointy jutting clumps of metal like knives that rip through clothing and skin, making you think about how they'll do that to you if you try to get out, so you stay in.

But when you're playing baseball and you're the power hitter you can send that little ball out over the homerun fence, like little parts of yourself escaping a few ounces at a time.

CAMP

For the end of summer there's a swim camp a few hours' drive north of London that girls from Michigan go to all summer.

Then they leave for the last week so that both boys and girls from Ontario can use it for a change.

It's just for fun, a goof-off. You wouldn't be training hard for anything at this point in the season when after it is two weeks off until the new swim season starts again in mid-September after school settles back in.

When I did it a couple of years ago I thought it was really serious but now I'm one of the oldest kids along with Hanley, he came too. Hanley's in such good shape for butterfly, the hardest stroke, and not usually one for distance because of how much energy you need to use for the legs—it really saps your strength—that he can swim it for distance, over a mile, all the way out to the rock island and back.

Hanley and I are way better than the other kids. We're the leaders. We're the doting mom and dad. We're exploring the boundaries of the lake in our canoe usually with a little kid in a life jacket along for the ride in the middle. At the same time, we're going along with what the coaches want and not being smarter.

Everybody thinks we should be together, boyfriend and girlfriend. I would never even think that. Isn't a boyfriend supposed to be someone better than you who would never want you even in a million years?

13

MATH CLASS

I love math class. You never have to study for it because there's nothing to memorize, either you get it or you don't. If you don't get it, you just figure it out.

Grade eleven math class is Jeff Bevan kitty corner and back to the left, Pete Poston behind him and Don Weaver to his left. It's Mr. Greene sometimes in a special tie with math equations stitched on it, behind thick silver aviator glasses making his eyes extra huge and blurry and the stuck inside your head and can't get out mad scientist kind of voice. He's walking fast in front of the blackboard with his chalk, almost dancing, excited.

Math class is warmth. It's being relaxed, like getting cooked slowly in a soup. Jeff Bevan's athleticism should make up for his not being as tall as me. He has scrunched-up eyes making you want to lean in closer to see what's going on inside of them, leading into an also scrunched nose. His standout feature is olive skin. Olive skin has a yellow undertone. Even though not the smartest at math he's going to keep at it until he gets it. Pete Poston is his closest friend. He's tall but with skinny, droopy shoulders, short on muscle fibre, making him look burdened. His mouth looks dark and cavernous from braces with elastics, exaggeratedly so because unfortunately it matches in darkness what otherwise would be handsome brown, tinged with green, eyes. Don Weaver isn't soft but he seems it. Because his eyes are kind of bulgy and faded-out blue but with the big curly eyelashes, kind of like movie star eyes. With his eyes, they're so dazzling you can't help but be pulled into them like a TV commercial but then the galaxy you go to turns out to be finite and not very mathematically inclined. He's the boyfriend of Mel Neal.

With all of them together, all friends, and because of that relating to each other warm and closely, I get to feel the feelings of being on the inside of them and especially him, Jeff, and liking it.

Mr. Greene has a student teacher this week, Mr. Wright. I'm getting attention making jokes about him being Mr. Right, as in the perfect guy. He's not so bad but he's not the amazing Mr. Greene with his power to hold together all the giddy focus. What I'm asking Mr. Wright is if maybe we could switch the

X and the Y axis. I think it makes more sense for the X axis to be going up and down and the Y axis side to side. Doesn't Mr. Wright?

ETCETERA

Mel Neal, whose boyfriend is Don Weaver, is also the best friend of Beatrice Lerner. They're both in math class too. Mel Neal and Beatrice Lerner being best friends doesn't make sense although everybody says they always were, because Beatrice is really smart and Mel is pretty and nice, but she's more like a near-sighted mouse even though she isn't actually near-sighted and doesn't wear glasses, with her cute pointy nose in the air trying to smell her way around and her faded eyes always looking a little small and lost and distracted.

Whereas Beatrice has the big, get-to-the-facts stare and does wear glasses, big ones. They both have long straight hair, but Beatrice's face is also splattered with big red pimples. Partly why the pimples stand out so much is her older sister. Beatrice's older sister, in grade thirteen, is gorgeous. She's the same as Beatrice but finer and with perfect skin and eyes and teeth, which if you look closely at Beatrice she is almost too. But then you remember you're only thinking that because of the comparison—really she's not like that at all.

CLIQUES

Beatrice Lerner and Mel Neal are also in the group I joined in grade nine only didn't know because they were in the opposite lunch just like Julie Pollard and I were; only they're all still friends.

Except now I'm going in another direction friends-wise. For instance Delilah George is my biology partner and what's growing in the Petri dish under our lab desk is the "cure for cancer." Suzie Pritchard has the same lab desk for her biology class so she's also adding ingredients for the "cure for cancer."

Our biology teacher Mr. Havelock has the little kind of voice that he can't push past the front row and it's not just his voice is like that. So he wouldn't be the one to notice our personal science experiment and then Delilah tells me she's going to be sitting at the front of the class now instead of with me because what we've been doing means she hasn't been studying much official biology lately. I can tell it's her father's idea by how her shoulders slump leading her body towards the front desk and not even considering my arguments otherwise.

I wouldn't have thought of that, going to the front to try harder. I don't get the point of biology. I don't know how I'm expected to be any good at it when I just don't get it.

OPPOSITE

The sad thing about biology that's going on at the same time as the "cure for cancer" is Jesse McIntyre who used to be my biology lab partner in grade nine at the same desk, except two classrooms down.

Both her parents and her older sister were killed on the highway. A person in the car driving in the opposite direction had a heart attack and lost control of his car so that it went into opposing traffic, which was a head-on collision killing a lot of Jesse's family.

I don't know why her parents didn't notice and pull away just in time. I don't know why it had to happen to Jesse because she was always so nice and perfect and didn't do anything wrong.

SYMPATHY

Delilah was in the same school as Jesse in grade school. So she called her on the phone to express her condolences. I wish I was good enough to do something like that. I feel so sorry for Jesse even though she never paid much attention to me.

WE'RE MOVING

For moving downtown, now that Cindy's in high school too, and it's what we all wanted for a while, first mom gets one of the kids on the swim team's dad, who's a small independent realtor, to sell the house. Because mom will always give the small guy she knows the chance. She's ready to be sold on his merits.

But at the same time, mom isn't going to get carried away. When the house doesn't sell, she's not afraid of hard feelings. So then she goes with a bigger company.

SPOOKIER

Cindy and I are so proud of our house. It's covered in ivy, has a big crabapple tree out front and the siding, the part that's not red bricks, is painted bright turquoise blue. I know that last part sounds possibly weird against the red brick but it looks really nice and mostly it is way more interesting than the other houses on the street. Behind the ivy and the crabapple tree and other trees too, it might look a little spookier than the other houses in our neighbourhood. What's so great to us is it's disguised to not be a house in the suburbs.

It's the fall so we're sitting in the living room opening our photo album on the hassock showing prospective buyers pictures of the crabapple tree blossoming in spring. But maybe all the things that we think are beautiful about the house are what are bad about it too.

How many people buying the house know that this is the house where my brother, who killed the girl, grew up? Maybe there's something about the house that makes them suspicious about it that we can't see, like it's somehow haunted. Is there a special area in the listing where it states the history of the residents of the home? Should there be?

Maybe it's hard to sell the house because of that. Maybe the only way we can sell it is for a bargain to someone who it doesn't matter to so much that the house had that darkness in it once or always or never did or does.

I feel so terrible leaving it behind. Like abandonment.

QUEEN

The reason why mom was the first baby born in the Gaspé hospital, which she's so proud of, even though back then most babies were born at home was because granny, her mom, hated the midwife, who was also her mother-in-law, so much. She thought the midwife was like the queen of a pack of vultures whose only thought was to take advantage of an opportunity to discover what was in between the dark place between her legs. Which was going to be my mom coming out. So granny went to the hospital to have my mom instead of that.

I think everywhere granny looked was a trap, even at the ocean. Because she was born lower down in the numbers in her family, because she was a girl, she didn't get to go to more school even if she knew she was smarter.

Then looking out the hospital window across the Gaspé harbour to where her brothers went out on their fishing boats each day, she got stuck with granddad and the baby.

So then she ran away. She left my mom and ran away.

HOPES ABOUND

The weekend of our moving house I'm away. I'm at nationals in British Columbia.

Nick Casteel and my coach Sean are hushed whispers, separate, at the back of the pull-out stadium benches, developing Nick's plan of what place finishes he needs to get, to have a chance to qualify for the "B" Canadian team, which gets to go on a trip to England.

I have just as good of a chance as Nick to make it on this team, if not better. I wonder why we're not talking about it too. Why is it that when there's a team to be made the only way I make it is if it's just by coincidence?

It's another one of those gloomy pools made of too much dark wood interior. There are hopes for me but they are not getting talked about. There are hopes all around me.

The most magnificent swimmer in Canada, Megan Cody, who's already won two Olympic medals, is here too. Something is bothering her. Her regular air of graceful beauty keeps cracking like a boy's voice beginning to change. Like who is going to be able to love her, who is going to be good enough for her greatness? She's trying to but can't keep private what's showing when she's talking to him, her new boyfriend, on the pool deck before her races or later, after standing for some more medals on the podium. He's a swimmer too, but not as good as her, so what's he going to tell her, what's he going to say to help her when it's hard enough swimming his own races not as good as her? She storms and flails, ready to break, isn't having a good swim meet, but still mostly winning everything.

SWEET ISOLATION

I think Sean's idea is that if you really want it, you're supposed to come up to him and say so. You're not supposed to have any inner doubts about if I assert myself as a swimmer and get known too well, is that going to reflect back on my family in a way that might not be so good after all. Or about the guilt of, do I even deserve to do well, after what happened and what can I do to fix it but I'm not supposed to be having this problem in the first place, this is a wrong problem.

Only, having all these problems is probably what makes me such a good candidate for all the swimming up and down and around so why can't he just give a little back, only I don't want to ask too much of anyone ever because isn't that what my brother did—want too much, want too much in the wrong way? So I have to assume Sean is right, only how exactly do I do what the secret message of his actions tells me what he wants me to do?

LET X EQUAL

The difference between Beatrice Lerner from math class and me is her older sister and my older brother. Since her older sister is so beautiful with the small nose and the perfect teeth and Jamie Rudman, the captain of the football team, Beatrice is only left with being the smart sister. So in math class she's top of the class but so am I because math is just to "get," and Mr. Greene is so funny, you can't miss it, I had him last year too.

The only thing for me is all the boys that make my eyes go soft and that softness spreads to the back of my head and around my shoulders and down into my heart and belly, which I love and have to have, even though it isn't right. It's wrong.

So it has to be it's not real. What I'm feeling in math class is not real. I know because the corollary is that if it was real I would be talking about it. I could do something about it. Conversely because it's not real, it's okay to be. No one's doing anything wrong. No one's getting hurt. What I'm figuring out is a different kind of math Mr. Greene isn't teaching. It's taking up the place the funny math on Mr. Greene's ties used to go.

REAL PERSONAL FAMILY HISTORY

What my mom says is that her very many greats grandfather, so the same for me but one more "great," was the adopted son of Sir Isaac Brock the hero of fighting off the United States from Canada in the War of 1812.

Cindy's like that too. She'll say things that sound completely made up. But then when she says something so ludicrous you decide to stop ignoring her for a moment to inform her, she'll go and prove it, it'll turn out to be something true.

Then after the war, he, the supposed adopted son, who had come over from Scotland to fight for Canada, was awarded a parcel of land in Gaspé for not getting killed and also to keep the French from getting too dominant in Quebec.

What I think is that since it's true Sir Isaac was very popular maybe he did say stuff like "You're like a son to me" to his men, the soldiers fighting under him. Only it would have to be someone from our family would take it literally and then all of them afterwards carrying it on forward like it really was true, even if it wasn't in the history books. Embellishing. When all the other soldiers would have just been smiling, saying to themselves, "What a nice sweet guy that Sir Isaac is," and letting themselves be consoled.

Except he wasn't a Sir yet. First he had to get killed.

BUILDING

My new friend Suzie Pritchard isn't coming to Driver's Ed with my other new friend Delilah George and me because she's actually a year younger since she accelerated past grade four and went to gifted school. She's not old enough yet to drive.

Suzie bought platform shoes she loved so much she wanted me to get some too. Platform shoes vary. These ones are an inch and a half of extra thickness under the length of the sole making you an extra inch and a half taller. They have a fancy strap that goes up and around your ankle. They're shimmery brown.

Suzie is very petite, which is why the shoes are fine for her. Suzie is also very convincing. I told her they would be of no use for me. I told her I'm already too tall.

It was very fun buying them with Suzie. After I wore them the first time looming over everyone like an apartment building I put them away. They're at the back of my closet, shimmering.

SQUEAL

The thing Delilah George laughs about the most in driving class is our teacher, Glenn Munson, mainly because of the cologne. After the classroom session, when he takes us out to practice driving, it is a very strong smell affecting the car atmosphere.

Delilah can't stop laughing about the irony of Glenn Munson. She thinks that because he is so homely-looking, with the thick glasses, the gnarled teeth, the kind of chin that is very close to the neck, that he should just give up. He shouldn't wear the sideburns. He shouldn't wear the turtleneck sweater to hide the bad chin. He should definitely forget about the cologne.

Her eyes go crazy small and squinty like a pig's and the sound of her laugh is a high-pitched squeal too.

STICK SHIFT

Suddenly dad realizes he better teach me how to drive a standard since the driver's course only taught how to drive an automatic, so that he can get a break in the morning and sleep in a little later.

Sunday morning, the A&P parking lot is empty, so we can take the red Honda Civic for a spin—press clutch, change gear—up and around, up and around. There's a little hilly spot right in the middle of the parking lot. Watching out not to crash into the lamp posts.

On the way home we stop at the Portuguese bakery on Adelaide for Portuguese buns, which is a new discovery in our new neighbourhood. These buns are crusty and really chewy. They're amazing.

COME BACK

Of course my mom couldn't possibly actually remember her mom leaving her when she was a baby and coming back later when she was still a baby, an older baby. No one remembers back that far. Why granny came back—I don't think there was anywhere else she figured out she could go.

Which is why my mom always acts like she's beyond criticism, why she never allows there to be a word said against her; she knows your complaints about her are a joke compared to what she got. Granny didn't come back for her.

STEALING

For morning practice, which is at the new L-shaped university pool now, I pick up Cassie Fowler from her house on the way to and drop her off on the way back.

We don't swim in the extra part of the L. It's a diving well. It's for divers.

After practice Cassie gets me to join her stealing from the wire baskets in the locker room containing the athletic gear of students and teachers from the university. If you have one of those baskets you should be sure to loop the straps of your bathing suit through the lock part otherwise people who like to steal can just pull the bathing suit out through the holes between the wires.

There's nothing extra with Cassie. She's like a knife. She is hidden because of the stealing but she's not worried about getting me involved and stealing with her and knowing. Even though I'm better than her at swimming, even though I'm the best swimmer on the team and the most looked up to, she can tell I won't tell. We're taking things and giggling.

Cassie has extra-long eyelashes but they're not curly and they're pale. She knows they're there. She's at the end of a string of a lot of Roman Catholic kids in her family. She has a hard, straight-arm swim style that suits her. She's fast.

She's the one who said Curt Kohl looked like a clown when he was acting like he had a crush on her.

14

SHINY GLOOM

Evening practice is still at Wolseley Barracks, which is a walk from school and then a wait in a big, empty, shiny sitting table section. It's shiny because even though the tables are at the back against the wall they face a big glass window area that lets a lot of light through to the shiny floor. Because it's the army they shine it a lot.

But where the tables are is kind of dark too. They sit at the beginning of a separate wide hall, on the edge of all that shiny light. Altogether it's shiny and gloomy.

I'm clowning around with Mr. Thompson who's the father of Jan and Greg Thompson, also Becky. Mr. Thompson's not a coach but gets involved by helping coach sometimes. He helped me improve my swim starts so that now I'm a fast starter. The Thompsons have been around swimming for a long time too. For example Jan is the girl who beat me for the all-around trophy at the city championships when I was ten. She's the only one who ever beat me. She's not that good anymore though.

Her older brother Greg used to be one of the bigger, better boys but he's in university now. When we were at swim camp last summer, because he's captain, when the compliments are coming in he's taking credit for the cheer our team made up in the cheer section of the competition, which he's right, it was outstanding and deserved to win. What I dislike is not being acknowledged, especially when I'm the one who came up with the rhymes and the idea about the leeches too.

They're also a funny family. Jan shows her humour by calling me by my middle name in a fun but possessive way, making me feel special. I don't know what Greg does but everyone's always laughing along with him and he's laughing too. Their younger sister, Becky, is another youngest sibling who belches. That's how she acts funny.

Naturally Mr. Thompson is funny too and I'm talking in a loud voice to keep up with him because after all he is an adult and has had more practice and I'm thinking I'm doing a pretty good job, life of the party.

ONLY

Mr. Thompson phones up my parents and tells them I was talking inappropriately about my father. My jokes weren't good. There was too much criticalness showing through, out in public.

My parents are very serious and they are sitting me down and talking to me and their decision is that I can't go to the swim meet this weekend in Guelph, which is a selection swim meet to make a team for a trip to British Columbia. Because my mom says I shouldn't talk about my dad that way and he's agreeing with her.

I can't believe they're doing this to me. I know things about them, I say, they're not so perfect. Mom is very quiet and wants to know what these things are. So now I'm thinking, what are the things my mom doesn't want me to know about? But all I know is, you know, what they're like, that this is the stupidest consequence ever, that my dad is a wimp and they both know it, and this is my mom's idea and my dad going along like always and what do they want from me?

Not to say anything even resembling what I think and to realize that that cheater Mr. Thompson, just like his deceiving, rhyme-stealing son, is on their side.

NICE

The good thing about it is maybe for Yvonne Nowak because even she makes the team to go to British Columbia but really I think she would have made it even if I had too, so nothing against her, I just think this team would have been really easy to make if Yvonne Nowak made it.

7-UP

In Gaspé the wetness in the wood of the cottage, which is a regular house too and can be lived in, in the winter, is the good wetness smell. You want to turn into a grub and wiggle your way down into that smell like's it's the cool earth surrounding you snug and tight.

Granddad has the back mudroom lined with cardboard pop-bottle boxes full of empty 7UPs to take back to the store. The latch on the screen door is the old kind that clinks when it shuts. The pop bottles make a different clink when you're jostling them around, organizing for taking back for nickels.

We're having turkey dinner only Cal wants the drumstick and so does Cindy and so does Aunt Sylvia. Aunt Sylvia still acts like a child sometimes since she's only eight years older than Cal. When you go outside from the argument it's the bleak kind of sun making the grass look white like it's a full moon at nighttime and the colours don't spread out as much as they should.

The graveyard of the small church is right next door but granny's not dead yet. She's inside serving turkey.

SICK BUNNY

Driving home from Gaspé, stopping at hotels along the way, we come to one with a hutch of cute little bunnies. I'm cuddling them and dad taking pictures so that by the time we're back home from staying at that high place on the Gaspé side of the mountains I don't feel like changing the hutch, cleaning up the rabbit droppings.

It's all seeming too regular and my arms don't want to reach up. They're numb like I slept on them funny. But I think my magic bunny that came to me from a magician noticed.

Because then when I go to him in the morning a lot of times he's on his side and can't get up unless I help him with the back feet toenails going scritch, scritch, scritch, pushing against the what-is-wrongness, trying to right himself.

AHEAD

The car dad's driving now is a baby blue Camaro. He's standing in our new driveway in our new-old house downtown with the little garden area at the top that a friend of mom's who's in landscaping put some nice trees and bushes in, with the cedar shavings around. He's going to work but it's not dark and six in the morning anymore because now he's going into a management job, not working as an electrician on the floor of the plant anymore. It's management and labour working together taking advantage of his union organizing know-how, how all the men like him, for the good of the company.

He's wearing jeans on the bottom and a brown corduroy suit jacket on the top, a casual yet professional look.

NEIGHBOUR

While I'm at swim practice and while mom is out jogging with our new across the street neighbour Carolyn, who was and still is my mom's customer, with three and then four kids even though she didn't start until she was thirty-eight, Cindy's looking after Carolyn's kids.

They're watching *Sesame Street* and drinking soymilk that is green, because of allergies to regular milk, in a small room off the back of the kitchen.

University professors must make a lot of money because you've never seen a kitchen or house more beautiful than Carolyn's whose husband is a university professor at Western while Carolyn is looking after the kids. Walking in the front door is the breeze at your back of going into always summertime.

Carolyn's husband likes to sit on the front porch that sweeps around the house at a small round table with French curly-cue chairs and his friends coming over. Every time I cross the street when he's there what he talks to me about is beautiful, tall, graceful, aquiline women with swimmers' bodies, which seems to be about me.

Well, obviously it is about me. I know he's really smart because he's a university professor so I'm not going to criticize him. I think what he thinks he's doing is humouring me. Like he thinks all I ever think about is how magnificent I am and how I look to him.

THE DESK

My mom's thing with him is how loud they can talk to each other. Carolyn must have told her something while they were jogging because my mom acts like she's smarter than him about it but also frustrated because somehow he can fight her back. Ammunition for how smart she is, is her bookstore and her business, which is going very strong and she's switching to a bigger location.

Also because of her antiquing side she has a very special oak captain's desk with a lot of interesting drawers he wants that will match perfectly with his being a professor. She's a wheeler-dealer waiting for him to offer her the right price.

GRACE

Carolyn is the real beautiful one even if her face is behind glasses and she looks a little shyly downwards. It's from all the kindness and smartness and easiness with her children even though she's not hiding what the work is to have four so close together. Also that she comes from rich American parents and was always spending her childhood summers on the ocean may mean she's actually the reason the house is so big and beautiful and always has that breeze when you go in.

And the way she moves. There's something free about the joints in her knees and her elbows when she bends down to pick up a stray red scooter or the empty garbage can at the bottom of the driveway on garbage day with the driveway itself all crumbly and disintegrating, but it's okay to have a driveway like that in this old neighbourhood. There's something unfettered.

DUMPY

Fortunately for him she's not that tall, maybe a little more than him, because really he's pretty short and dumpy.

I would never have said that if he didn't always say that about himself.

I actually don't even think it myself.

The way he acts is: he goes in and out of the house to sit and read at his round table on the verandah like he's a nervous mole going in and out of his mole hole.

MONEY

What's nice for me is that even though I was only sixth at nationals last summer I made a really hard time, the Olympic qualifying time, in the two hundred backstroke, which means that now I'm a nationally carded athlete so the government sends me extra money to pay for all the extra costs that go along with being a competitive swimmer.

I'm using the government money to pay for the next trip I'm going on to nationals, to Regina, which is also the meet for picking the Canadian team that's going to the Commonwealth games.

SPOTLIGHT

I get to be the main picture in the paper for Commonwealth games hopefuls. There's two guys who have a better chance than me that the paper's talking about first and it says they're on our team, but really they're two of the guys from Waterloo.

So putting my picture in, it's a picture of me just swimming along doing freestyle, breathing to the side with my arm above my head about to enter the water and my eyes looking down so they look like they're closed, you just see the eyelashes, respects the fact that a native London person really should get the spotlight ahead of some Waterloo guys who happen to be swimming for London.

ARMPITS

I wish it didn't have to be a picture of my big armpit though. I'm trying to decide if my armpit is ugly or not. It's inevitable if you're going to be a half-decent swimmer that you're going to have big shoulders. It's a given.

Armpits like that don't look ugly on a guy. They look nice. But who would like a girl who looked like that?

I am glad I'm looking down in the picture though. At least that makes me look a little demure. Would anyone think I look pretty?

HOW I KNOW

The newspaper article says my coach Sean sees me as the next most hopeful chance after the Waterloo guys, that I have a real chance of making the Commonwealth team.

BROTHERS

I'm doing this thing with hairclips to my hair that gives me bangs. If I comb the front part down hard when it's wet, don't touch it and let it dry that way, the hair will stay down and not ferociously fly up into curls. Then if I clip the side parts back they won't fluff up and ruin the effect. I've never had bangs before.

From inside I like to see the soft bits of hair when I look up. It makes me feel warm and soft especially in combination with looking at Tom Kohl, Curt Kohl's older brother, in the bright of the bus from the hotel on the way to the dark pool but I don't care if it's a dark pool anymore, I'm done with not liking dark pools; it means nothing.

The reason it's Tom Kohl is Curt Kohl wasn't good enough to come to Regina but then somehow his brother is coming with us even though he barely trains with us. The way Tom's different from Curt is he's got big bulgy bug eyes, while Curt's are big too but more settled-in looking. Tom's have more blue in them than Curt's. And they're glassy. He gets little red strawberries in his cheeks and his lips purse but not prissily—intently.

Since Tom is the first brother, Curt should really be in reaction to him but since I know Curt first I'm always thinking of Tom as the reaction. Like how Curt's slinky quietness turned into Tom's ready to burst out quality. Tom's pop eyes are all abstract-looking like a cat and dog are playing chase in the back of his head and when he looks out that's all he can see.

Tom's never going to say anything to me just like Curt never did. I wish my hair clips had little sharp points on their ends. Then what I could do is take one of the clips off, walk over to him on the bus on the way to the Commonwealth games trials and pop open one of his bulging blueberry eyes. Only it wouldn't be all blood and loss of perception leaking out, it would be words—words he would say to me.

COMPETITION

We also have Marci Bond, who's a bit younger than me, whose best event is the same as mine, as part of the team. She's tall, same as me, but her body is sleeker and with bigger feet. Supposedly having big feet is a bonus for swimmers.

I'm considering being intimidated by her suntan. It's from her training at a special swimming high school in Florida because of her parents' richness. Even though she's from London and good enough to make nationals, I've never seen her before.

Marci has an ugly stroke. The top of her arms slap the water like her every forward motion is an angry defeated protest but she doesn't realize it. It's from her ugly splashing up the mangled crowded swimming lanes in sunny Florida.

I try to think about beating her but her form appalls me too much to care the way I'm supposed to which of us is better.

THE UNDERNEATH POSITION

Dad's new job's not working out. I know why. It's because he doesn't know how to be in the position of being on top and everyone not liking you anymore because you can't just keep going along, you have to say what you want. He's going back to where he was before, getting up at six o'clock and organizing from within. That's how he likes it. He's going back to no brown corduroy suit jacket for working for management representing labour.

His baby blue Camaro's not in our driveway anymore. In a way it's perfect it's a Camaro because it's the first time he ever had such a sporty car, which goes with him being single now. Your dad's car can just drive out of the driveway one day with your dad in it and not drive back because of the way it's been for so long but pretending it wasn't.

Our parents don't say anything to me and Cindy besides it's happening. They're separating. That there's nothing to say proves everyone knows that in certain ways stopping pretending is really simple.

15

DAD

Men have a certain smell. How I know is I can smell the smell of that smell being gone. Maybe the smell has to do with the short whiskers from shaving that used to line up in swirl patterns from where the water left them beside the tap nozzle of the bathroom sink. Because they're not there anymore either.

SAMANTHA

The girl I've been hanging out with the most lately at swimming is done. Her shoulders always hurt even after two operations.

She holds them all the time, rocking back and forward, and scrunches her face to show the pain. She's so cute. Guys love her. She has a teddy bear voice and big empathetic brown eyes only she's laughing at the same time and you're included.

The problem is it's hard for her to really look in pain because of the cute face. She gets this little wrinkle between her eyebrows. Her face is serious but then her eyes look up at you through the wrinkle and then the tragedy turns in on itself and is laughing. But then she's not laughing anymore, she's crying, because of the way her shoulders are hurting her.

What we used to do together last summer was a "combining physical features" game. We would pick which one of us we decided had the best of a specific feature. Then we would explain to the guys how we were making the perfect physical self out of our two selves. The game idea is an example of how Samantha would be able to find a way to be both "cute to guys" and engage the wit and humour of a girlfriend, making it all the more fun and interesting for everybody.

It would be at Thames the outdoor fifty-metre pool that we were better at, both having the long, strong kind of stroke technique. The sky would be really sunny but with the pool right there to get into if you needed. We were always choosing my nose because hers was kind of knobby but now I think we should have picked my whole total face and none of hers because if her shoulders were hurting her that much maybe my face would have showed it.

LEMONADE FLAVOURED

Before we moved and we were still living in the suburbs I had to ride my bike much farther to and from summer swim practice two times a day so on the way home I would buy lots of popsicles to quench my thirst. But popsicles melt fast especially on hot summer days so I would arrange my bike route home for stopping at select convenience stores spaced the right intervals apart for when I was ready to buy my next popsicle.

Only my favourite was white popsicles, which is lemonade-flavoured, but not very many stores sold them so I would have to buy two at this one particular store and eat them really quickly before the second one melted.

It was a store on Maitland in the old part of the city with lots of trees giving nice shade for riding your bicycle with no hands, or one hand depending, and slurping popsicles along the way.

PUSHING

Swim practice is starting up again for fall. I'm in the fast lane with the guys but not the guys from Waterloo who if things go the same as the last two years won't show up again until the spring. I can see Bessie Bauman with her bathing cap covering up her red hair and her spidery stroke two lanes down pushing to arrive. Or she might turn out like her brother with only her legs in the pool, sitting out the tough sets, rubbing ice on her shoulders. Bessie and Travis also have an older sister who has breasts because she was never too serious about swimming so she got them.

What happens if you're a girl and you're training for four hours a day at swimming is you get shoulders instead of breasts. It's not like you get absolutely no breasts, it's just they're not going to be that big. What's beautiful is that if you're a girl with big shoulders you really don't want to have big or even regular breasts because it looks bad. It's a bad combination. It's not aesthetic.

Think of a guy with fairly muscular arms and shoulders and imagine him with big breasts. See what I mean? It looks all wrong. If you have big breasts and big shoulders it emphasizes the big shoulders even further. So that's the beauty of it.

Bessie's shoulders are getting big and she's going to be in the fast lane with me soon. Actually right now Bessie's doing her repeats faster than me. Today I'm not keeping up too well with the regular guys in my lane. I'm struggling getting in the mood.

DIRECTION

My coach Sean says to me, "If you're not going to put more effort into it than that, just leave until you're ready to come back." Like that. Pretty tough. Maybe it means I'm supposed to snap to it and tell him no, I want to stay and will train harder. Maybe it means I'm supposed to come back tomorrow with the right attitude. But it feels good walking out of the bright white wall tiles pool with its no windows looking out; its shut-in voice echoes.

BENCH

One time Sean came to practice with a dark beard shadow, scratched the workout on the board and stayed the entire practice lying on his back on the bench. Sometimes his legs would be off the end of the bench slanting down to the ground. Sometimes they would be bent making an upside down V of his lower half, with the feet on the bench. He had his arm over his eyes.

Being a coach is a weird job because you have to get up so early in the morning, then do nothing all day, then work again in the evening.

We just kept along swimming our practice. If you think we looked in each other's eyes and gave each other the "this is kind of strange" look we didn't really. It was just a quieter than usual practice.

FEEL

Sean also had this bursting-out feel to him, not fat but maybe he could be if he didn't watch out. He walked kind of athletic, putting extra emphasis on his thighs, springy, running shoe wearing. He would hold his hands in fists while he walked along the side of the pool coaching, with the thumbs in, which also made it look like he was flexing his arm and shoulder muscles.

Once he was mad at the team for doing badly at an out of town swim meet. So the next day of the meet to make him feel better about how we cared and could show team spirit we did this big elaborate ceremony before the racing started in front of all the other teams, spectators and officials. We paraded in a line to the side of the pool. The guy whose idea it was held a clear container of water high over his head, which was supposedly from our pool but was actually tap water he got from the boys' change room before coming out on deck, and poured it into the pool we were competing in, signifying bringing the power of our pool to it.

On the way home in the van in the dark—the team rents a van or two for us to travel together in—Sean was giving me that appreciating, looking at you for who you are, wondering look from his eyes. I think he must have liked our ceremony. I was singing along with the rest of the kids, it was a sing-along, feeling warm and showing myself like a cat on your lap who lets you rub its belly for a change.

SCIENTIFIC NEWSFLASH MOON

Scientists are still seriously debating over the origins of the moon. Even they don't get how it got where it is or whether it even belongs. One theory is the earth getting into a big cataclysmic collision with a Mars-sized body early in its formation and then the moon made partly out of earth getting extracted out of it.

SOUTH

Delilah George convinced me to quit Central and go to South, which is a semester school, with her. It wasn't hard. If I go to a semester school I can finish high school with all my credits a whole year ahead. I'll be done high school.

But Suzie Pritchard is going to stay at Central. Also coming to South are Delilah's friends Sally Talbot and Hillary Kerr who are both moved out from their parents because of not getting along with them and sharing an apartment near school.

I already met Hillary a few times last year at a different apartment she lived in, already moved out from her parents. She was living near Grace Fries' house.

THE OPPOSITE OF HILLARY KERR

All my life I was always seeing Grace Fries' house on the corner, on the way to swim practice, a big tall house with the brick painted white with bright yellow shutters on the side of all the windows to perk it up. It was like a famous house. It was Grace's.

Grace Fries is looking through her eyelashes, slow on the uptake, when she's beginning to take French horn beside me in music class when we're in grade nine together. She's adopted, her skin is darker and her mother is one of my mother's customers. I'm better because I already know what to do from playing French horn for two years, since grade seven, in grade school.

By the time I'm visiting Hillary, Grace is in band and I'm thinking how Grace would have done it slowly, in one of the rooms on the other side of the famous yellow shutters. Muffled French horn sounds pressing out the slightly open window, but held in gently until she's ready by the tall, tall trees around.

ANARCHY

At Hillary's I give her one of my wallet-size school pictures I just got back from photo day, what school pictures are for, giving them to friends in your group. Of course I already gave one to Delilah.

Hillary is from the country, Clinton, and used to be so homely but then along came punk rock. Then her big cracked lips, pointy chin and cold green translucent eyes she looks away with, laughing—smirking smarter than you and loving reading Dostoyevsky—turned beautiful.

Hillary tapes my wallet-size school photo of my bleached curly hair from chlorine and my red suspenders for a unique fashion statement and my rosy cheeks, smiling like I do belong and everything is going to be okay, on the outside of her apartment door for everyone to look at coming in. I see myself. It's there next time I visit Hillary with Delilah. Surrounding it Hillary draws thick black magic marker arrows pointing at it saying "Anarchy."

NOT HURTING MOON

Because of there being less gravity on the moon than on earth, when Neil Armstrong and Buzz Aldrin got up there, the first men on its surface, what they weren't afraid of was getting hurt from falling down. They threw themselves around like children playing in water at the beach. They jumped high like dogs catching Frisbees.

The moon would just be letting them. It wouldn't do anything mysterious or unexpected. It would behave according to the normal laws of science. For example Armstrong's first impression was of its fine powdery surface.

Then when they left, the moon wouldn't be longing for their return watching them flying away in their funny metal machine the sun glinted off of when they were finished with it.

FUNERALS

For granny's dying, it was a while after it happened they told me. The reason they waited I could tell by how they were acting was because of taking into consideration the problem of my sensitivities, all my crying. I couldn't stop myself. Not that it was wrong of me and anyone could be mad at me, more the annoyance of putting up with someone very childish, because in our family we keep those kinds of feelings to ourselves. We manage them.

There must have been a funeral. Mom must have gone. When did they go?

For Selena, naturally I didn't go to Selena's funeral. You don't go to the funeral of the person someone in your family killed even if it was all just a big mistake maybe no one could have done anything about; we didn't know it was going to happen—that there was something about the way our family was, was going to make it happen.

NEW APARTMENT

Fortunately Hillary's new apartment doesn't have the photo taped on the door anymore. Sally Talbot, her roommate's problem is she just had her genital warts removed and she has to go two weeks without vaginal sex so do we have any fun ideas for her for what to do with her boyfriend, he's a bass player in a band, for the next two weeks.

Sally's way of talking is she says the first "a" in vaginal, really long and drawn out, making it sound like it's a different word from what it is, not private, like it could be a regular word you're used to seeing on your mom's grocery shopping list on the fridge. We're squeezed in at the kitchen table, the kitchen window over our heads somewhere for looking out of. What's being talked about involves the shower, which is in the bathroom off the hallway of Hillary and Sally's apartment.

CLOTHING

Sally likes to dress up. All the kids in class are staring at her unique appearance but she just stays with a serious "I'm paying attention to the lesson" look on her face, a contradiction because you expect a kid dressed like that to also be drawing attention to herself and being disruptive in class. But then that's how she makes it so that her very serious attitude seems unique and special too.

She's lucky she's so petite because there are so many good clothes at the Goodwill for you if you're petite. Sally used to wear tidy t-shirt tops, the kind with a few buttons at the collar, and short tennis skirts when she was a regular girl towards the outside of a regular clique, because of being over-talkative and over-agreeable, when she went to Central. Now sometimes Sally's a flapper from the twenties. Sometimes she's a hippy from the sixties. She likes to wear lots of necklaces together at the same time.

For Delilah, her problem to work around is she's overweight but she finds a men's navy wool coat, down to below her knees with a soft high collar, double breasted with the buttons spaced far apart. By her look at herself in the mirror I can tell she sees her big bosom in the man's coat is working perfectly, contradictorily, sexily. It's her signature coat. Too bad spring has to come.

Delilah likes to go out to the smokers' area at school and lean against the wall in her sleek blue coat, squint her eyes into the cold sun and blow the smoke out in one slow steady stream. When it gets to spring, she likes to tilt her head back and shake her hair so she can feel it on her neck and shoulders.

My problem is bigness, especially big shoulders, so women's stuff hardly ever fits. My Goodwill look gets to be men's fifties-style straight leg pants and men's bright-coloured button-up shirts.

DIRECTIVES

One of Suzie Pritchard's favourite words is insightful. Her plan is to one day be a writer, but not just a regular writer, an insightful writer.

Compared to me my sister is not very insightful. When we're in the breakfast nook together, which is an add-on section to the kitchen, all windows with panes, looking out on the garden and the pool, and Cindy's having her boiled egg, old-fashioned style in an egg cup, the top of the shell peeled open, dipping toast in the runny yellow, I'm the one mom is listening to for insights. Cindy is used to being in the background.

This time I'm bringing up some of my thoughts on Cal and the possibility of his being trustworthy. Then Cindy decides to take a turn. She has the opposite view, which is, you should be closed to him. He's not. He's not trustworthy. There's a few other words mixed in rounding it out more.

Mom's having her eggs poached style with salt and pepper and also with soft yolks. She agrees with Cindy. Mom emphasizes that on this particular occasion Cindy is making some very important observations. She believes Cindy's insights in this instance might even be more insightful than mine.

GOING OUT

We're dressed up in our Goodwill clothes walking from Hillary and Sally's place to downtown. It's a biting cold spring night.

The ground is still hard, so we're being careful not to trip on the higher tufted frozen grass bits.

We think we look pretty good.

We're not old enough but they're not checking ID and still letting us into the Blue Boot to watch Sally's boyfriend's band's final set. What you do is get in the middle of the dance floor and jump up and down in the strobe lights. That's it. It's the pogo. Some people are very rough when they do it though, which is why it's a challenge. I'm going to stand on the sides.

16

AFFRONT

Friday night the principal calls from Central saying Cindy has to be brought home. He's saying it in a caustic way but also with the force behind it of don't bother trying to stop him because it's in his nature to take it like a personal affront, her being the way she is, drunk—a mess of unconsciousness sprawled on his office floor. So now Cindy has to come to South too so I can continue my job of being such a good influence on her.

One time Cindy has the car and she's pulling out of the school parking lot and, wham, she smacks the side of the car right into a pole in the middle of the parking lot. Then she's crying her eyes out, so upset.

The reason it looks familiar I'm realizing is because it must be her version of how I looked to her that time. What Cindy's missing when she's practicing her emulation of me are a couple of subtle differences between our accidents. When I got in my car accident I was responsibly driving home from swim practice. When Cindy crashed the car she was probably completely stoned. I was making a lane switch into my blind spot in moving traffic and it turned out not to even be my fault. Cindy hit a stationary object in a parking lot.

Cindy is the blind spot—of my mom anyway, because mom falls for it every time. Maybe mom believes her but Cindy would be doing herself a big favour by never considering going into acting.

GETTING IN

Cindy gets in because she's small so the boys don't mind her and then she's talking to them. She's measurable. She could never be spooky even when her lungs are turning black smoking out in the back of the school with them. She could never be intimidating. She's getting in even more.

OTHER NEIGHBOURS

Our next-door neighbours hate us. Because it's downtown it's a mixture. There are rental units that get rundown-looking, which is what our house used to be. Then there's like what our house is now. Nice. Fixed up. Then there are even more gorgeous houses, practically mansions like the Walters', Carolyn and Peter's, across the street.

The next-door neighbours' is a two-storey house turned into a duplex with two rental units one on each floor but it still looks in quite nice condition. They're on the main floor and like to sit out on the porch but they are both really ugly. The problem is trying to decide who is uglier. I think it's her. But there's something gorgeously juicy about her ugliness too.

It's her head. She has a big round pumpkin head but with a really flat face. Sometimes pumpkins do really grow like that. Her face is pasty white. She wouldn't look so ugly if she didn't always have a disgusted look on her face. Her mouth is turned down with the pointy teeth showing like a grimace. Her nostrils are permanently flared.

I don't know why they're always so upset with us other than we exist and go in and out of our house. Their house sits a little higher up on the land than ours and is fairly close so they're always looming. They must also be mad because our house is so pretty and it's ours.

What's strange is they have a daughter who's a little older than me and has the same flat pumpkin-face head and fair skin as her mother plus with super-plucked eyebrows arched up exaggerating the great expanse of face. But she has a pretty and slim body that doesn't look all rigid and stiff and puffed-up like theirs. It moves adroitly through them, delicate like a bat catching bugs at dusk. She's practically beautiful. I don't understand how having that daughter around wouldn't soften them, make them take it a little easy on their hatred of us.

One thing I like about them is they don't hate us because

of what Cal did. I just know they don't know about that because they're so ignorant and mean even without that. So there's nothing to hide from except regular hate.

BABY BLUE SWEATER

Mom is so happy with me because she just told me she's a lesbian in the upstairs hallway. It's not really a hallway. It's just a central square where her bedroom, my bedroom, the spare bedroom, the study, which is really the room where we watch TV but we don't watch TV that much, and the bathroom all meet in a big square.

When we moved into the house I picked my room right away. It's the front room above the porch that looks out to the Walters' house across the street, so it has the roof of the porch section in front of it, which at first didn't have the little railing posts around it because it wasn't fixed up all the way yet but does now, restored to its original form.

So Cindy's wasn't as good really, remote, an extra room on the back of the house, down this little flight of stairs, kind of cold in winter because it has lots of windows. But then her room turned out maybe even nicer than mine. She calls it the tree house because in the summer it's up amongst the leafy walnut tree branches. We put a pool in the backyard so it's also magically floating above the water too. It's like her personal oasis.

But what's so nice about my room is that I get to watch our other next-door neighbour Jay Griffin when he drives in his driveway at the end of the day every day. First he was friends with Peter Walter sitting on the front porch across the street with him all the time. Then he moved in next door with his wife and little girl. Then his wife left him and his daughter was visiting sometimes. Because of my window I saw the whole thing.

Mom's being a lesbian doesn't matter. It works out okay for me. I'm thinking of how I can add it to the list in my head of what is so unique about me a little way down after what my brother did. It's like I'm looking in the mirror trying on a new hat. She's so happy she reaches into the linen closet and there's a baby blue wool sweater in there, hidden, for a present for me for down the road, the kind with the design around the collar I like. But she's giving it to me now. So it's a new sweater I'm trying on, not a hat.

MONTY PYTHON

Suzie Pritchard's parents are so stupid. We go up to her room to smoke dope and then come down to the TV room and watch Monty Python with them, all cozy. Can you imagine how much that is making us giggle? Then they're only thinking how silly we are like we're just regular silly girls and not completely wasted. With Suzie's parents you don't feel bad when you're doing things you know they would consider wrong in front of them. You have no concern for their feelings.

At my house if I come home stoned I am so afraid I will get caught. Pretend to be normal and stay a million miles away, is what I say to myself to keep myself calm. It feels like I'm squeezed up into the left corner ceiling of the room. I am so certain my mom must know but is thankfully leaving me alone to creep to the safety of my bedroom.

SEDUCTION

Delilah's helping Suzie seduce a guy who lives two blocks up the street from Suzie on the second floor of a tenement house, which is another kind of house in the downtown neighbourhood. We have one three doors down from us too.

He has long brown curly hair in ringlets. He gets a four o'clock shadow because of the incredible manly potency of his facial hair growth. He's the picture Suzie has on her wall of Adam reaching out to God in the Sistine Chapel. I think I saw him in the distance once.

If Suzie's parents call wondering where she is, Delilah tells them she's there with her or some other excuse she thinks of on the spot if she needs to. The plan involves Delilah having to stay in close contact with Suzie and both of them having to be flexible for possible contingencies.

AURAS

Suzie and Delilah are seeing auras. I'm trying to see theirs too by squinting my eyes and looking for a light around the skin of their bodies. Suzie and Delilah say that's how you do it. They say mine is baby blue.

Except I don't want to have a baby blue aura. A baby blue aura sounds like someone boyish and co-operative, not the way I want to have to be. I don't want my aura to be the same colour as the car my dad left in, the sweater my mom gave me when she told me she was a lesbian, the swim team in Thunder Bay I could have left home for and joined if I really wanted to make it.

GETTING IN AND OUT

Visiting Cal, me on my side of the back seat of the car and Cindy on hers promoted from the lump in the middle, there would always be open countryside on the right side of the car going in and on the left side going out, desolate like how it must have looked landing on the moon the first time. It would be the same at the grounds of Oak Ridge where Cal was, a sweeping driveway alongside another expanse of view, still and bleak, that made you hear the crows cry.

We would never go into Penetanguishene itself. The good thing about always keeping the openness to one side of you and not going into town is the feeling that you can get out if you need to, you're not trapped. You can escape.

Also going into town would mean if we looked into the people's faces maybe they would be able tell who we were, what we were doing in town, visiting my brother incarcerated in a mental institution. It's nice to give yourself a break after going into it and through all the security and not having to look at another person who's maybe thinking that about you.

Plus why would we want to go into town? To get a treat at the convenience store? A bag of Ruffles potato chips or some red licorice? We didn't feel like a treat.

BUG VOICE

Unfortunately I have to take another course, I'm going to take it during summer school, to graduate high school because I couldn't do grade twelve math. It wasn't like grade eleven and I was getting worse at math because of too many interfering feelings, especially towards Jeff Bevan, getting in the way and there being no way of being able to do anything about them.

The problem is the grade twelve math teacher talks in this little scratchy bug voice. He's looking at you with his grey eyes from the front of the class like he's perfectly normal but then the marks he makes on the board are like bug transcription too. It's like I'm sitting there a big loud noisy girl in a bright pink dress and holding a skipping rope and putting the apple on his desk but he can't see it. He can't find me. We can't get through to each other.

When I go to the office and tell them I'm giving up on math class, I feel like I'm faking that I can't do it and everyone knows. Like any of them might look at me and say, "You just don't want to do it, admit it!" So what I do to be more convincing is squish myself into that shrunken-down bug state of how you have to be, to be inside the numbers like counting pool lengths to going nowhere and nothing and no one and when I get there, act bewildered. Then when they look at me with their magnifying-glass eyes it's all real. They can see me flailing, an infinitesimal white flag attached to one of my antennae in the universal sign of surrender, evidently for bugs too, like I really do get that I don't get it.

FRENCH

French is the same. I can't relate to the teacher. If I could it would help me take an interest in figuring out the past perfect verb tense. It's like he speaks another language. At least in French I can feel the dark closing in around me, like I have a chance to survive. Math is like the brightness of already being on the other side.

ANOTHER SUBJECT

One time I went to economics so stoned I was playing X's and O's with the girl beside me, Diana Davies, and it wasn't until the end of class when I was coming out of it that I realized she kept beating me exactly the same way every time.

She must have been getting very bored with me.

SAXOPHONE PLAYER

I'm coming home in the car from taking acid. Delilah gave it to me—a little orange pill you put under your tongue. We were planning to go to a bar to see a band. In the band Delilah was going for the saxophone player and Suzie was going for another guy not in the band, in another band, but who would be at the bar.

I wasn't going for anyone. I could only think of a guy at school Delilah noticed, so I did too, who was smart and a little edgy and I could get the idea of feeling a connection with him like a black streak between us.

CURB

When you're driving and you're high on acid, which you never took before, you lose your sense of direction. I do. You don't know where you are. You're afraid. So don't panic. Stop treating everything like it's a race to win. Pull over to the curb and wait and try to think of a way out of it. Try to think of a way around an entire dimension dropping out of the world, the one that keeps it all together and organized.

There is a solution. The solution is Suzie because Suzie has no sense of direction. So imitate Suzie. The way Suzie drives and knows where to go is based on an accumulation of knowledge of landmarks. So pull away from the curb and get myself home that way, from pushing really hard to remember where I am from where I've been.

Only being that way hurts because you look at things so hard like a rose bush beside the four wooden steps up to a porch with an empty hanging swing, like the large expanse of lawn at a corner by a stop sign. They keep on at you, more of them and their particulars in the night and they'll still be there tomorrow the same way and they stick in your head, nailing you into each other and won't go away, like being haunted.

AN ACTUAL CAT

I planned eating the Froot Loops out ahead of time because of my mom's being away on a trip to British Columbia and she only allows us eating healthy cereals in our house like Shreddies and Rice Krispies. They were sitting waiting for me on the kitchen counter. Except on my way into the house through the back gate, I get distracted by it. It's our swimming pool. The swimming pool is alive, all bluey gloppy wet and sloshing. Pulsing. In the pool things weren't that different on acid. I'm used to how the water makes your body zigzag in and out when your head is on the outside and you look down through it. Except for the hating-the-cat part. And the hating-the-cat not making any sense. Just the gnawing of it. The fact of the cat being Cindy's making me wonder if my feelings about Cindy were that infected that they were extending to her cat.

I would never pee in a pool. Opening the door to the house to get to the bathroom I realize what it is. It's only the cat wanting in the house, the cat scratching and nagging at the back of my brain. What I thought was me hating the cat was just the irritating feeling of the cat wanting to get in the house. Cats!

CONDUCTIVITY

Then our neighbour Jay Griffin comes over for a swim. Jay's allowed to come over anytime because of being friends with us, because of being friends with my mom. Jay helped my dad put in the fence posts when my dad was building the fence for around the pool.

Jay has this way of walking on his feet like they're very sensitive and hurt him. Like he's the monster or the beast that got the thorn but then he just kept on that way. He never met the princess who was supposed to take it out for him.

He gets in the shallow end. I'm already in the other end, the deep end. Did you know that water is a conductor and not just in science class, in real life? For example one time I was touching a plant, which is almost all made of water, and got a shock. But it was a completely different shock. It wasn't dry and short like a regular one. It was deeper. It was all rich and wet and amplified like a cry in a stairwell.

So I could feel how Jay was feeling about me from his end of the pool really well. And it was desire. And when I put my arm up to hold on to the diving board above my head, in this kind of aware way because it was like he could feel me feeling him and it was like he wanted me to do that and I was watching and feeling him to see what would happen, I could feel his desire-of-me surge come on extra-strong like the holding in of it was going to kill him.

Then, pretty abruptly, he went back next door to his house.

I went in to have my Froot Loops and let the cat out because this time the cat was on the inside of the door wanting out.

RACING

One time I was racing Kelly Hines at the Oktoberfest meet in Kitchener in the one hundred freestyle, a sprint. We were dead even, racing to the finish. I was going as hard as I could and I was flying and getting this feeling of the thrill of the race. I didn't hate Kelly. I loved her. I felt so powerful I didn't care who won.

Then I kept feeling that way for a long time after the race was over. And I was wondering why feeling that way was so unusual. I hardly ever felt that way.

STREETCAR

Delilah and I had to do a scene from a modern play for drama. Delilah's very into the performing arts so she picked *A Streetcar Named Desire* and played the really dramatic character, the one played by Vivien Leigh. I'm the boring wife. For my part, what I have to do is look at a picture of my husband, which in the scene we staged I do by taking a photograph out of my purse, and tell her how much I love him. Only, since acting that way really isn't my style I put a picture of my pet rabbit in it, from when he was alive, the one I got from the magician, to help me get in the mood.

Can you imagine what would have happened if suddenly, in the middle of the performance of the scene, I realized how immature it is to use a picture of your pet rabbit from when you were a kid to keep you in character in a love scene? It almost did happen.

I can't believe I did that. And Delilah! She was talking about it later with some other kids in the class, laughing like she couldn't believe she let me do that either. It could have broken her character too.

UNLIKE

I couldn't decide whether I should get graduation pictures or not. Because coming to South isn't really like graduating. Because of finishing off a year early and only being at the school for the one year and not knowing the kids in the school that well, so it's not really like you're in a graduating class.

Then I thought my mom would like it if I got the pictures, so I went to get them done and the photographer said he knew me from when I was a baby. He was a friend of our across the street neighbour Eunice in our old neighbourhood before we moved. Then I was wondering if he knew about me and our family and what had happened and feeling a little paranoid.

What he did wonder about was what had happened to my red hair like losing my red hair was what had happened to me. I said I don't have red hair. I never had red hair. But he insisted I did so that I started to think he might be right and if he was right maybe I still did have red hair and maybe I should go take a quick look in the mirror to make sure of what the situation was. Of course I didn't. Most likely it was just him remembering my mom having red hair and because my hair was reddish, which it still is, thinking I was going to have red hair.

So I posed with the graduation gown, holding the red plastic graduation roses but when we got the sample photos to choose from my mom said, "Why did you get these done?" Not for any bad reason, but because my head in the pictures just wouldn't get itself to belong with the gown and the roses and the graduation.

The expression on my face lurked above the flowers like a savvy criminal. It wouldn't fit.

Acknowledgements

Friends, especially Una, Jayne, Amy and Freedom.

The beautiful kids Jacob and Elijah.

Readers and appreciators at various stages, Deb Simmons, Ric Knowles, Constance Rooke, Alana Wilcox, Ruth Zuchter.

Margaret Christakos and the Influency gang.

Joan Guenther for a lot.

Stuart Ross, the very good editor, and Denis De Klerck for making it real.

My love Larry Eisenstein, for every bit of it—the living the loving the learning—gratitude.

Paula Eisenstein is a grown-up woman who lives in Toronto with her husband, son, and the vitally necessary two cats for families with writers in them. She was born and came of age in London, Ontario, and received her Bachelor of Arts from Mount Allison University. If a teacher were making comments about Paula on a report card, the teacher might say: Paula fails to understand the difference between fiction and non-fiction.

Other Books from Mansfield Press

Poetry

Leanne Averbach, *Fever*
Nelson Ball, *In This Thin Rain*
Stephen Brockwell & Stuart Ross, eds., *Rogue Stimulus: The Stephen Harper Holiday Anthology for a Prorogued Parliament*
Diana Fitzgerald Bryden, *Learning Russian*
Alice Burdick, *Flutter*
Alice Burdick, *Holler*
Margaret Christakos, *wipe.under.a.love*
Pino Coluccio, *First Comes Love*
Gary Michael Dault, *The Milk of Birds*
Pier Giorgio Di Cicco, *The Dark Time of Angels*
Pier Giorgio Di Cicco, *Dead Men of the Fifties*
Pier Giorgio Di Cicco, *The Honeymoon Wilderness*
Pier Giorgio Di Cicco, *Living in Paradise*
Pier Giorgio Di Cicco, *Early Works*
Pier Giorgio Di Cicco, *The Visible World*
Salvatore Difalco, *What Happens at Canals*
Christopher Doda, *Aesthetics Lesson*
Christopher Doda, *Among Ruins*
Rishma Dunlop, *The Body of My Garden*
Rishma Dunlop, *Lover Through Departure: New and Selected Poems*
Rishma Dunlop, *Metropolis*
Rishma Dunlop & Priscila Uppal, eds., *Red Silk: An Anthology of South Asian Women Poets*
Ollivier Dyens, *The Profane Earth*
Jaime Forsythe, *Sympathy Loophole*
Carole Glasser Langille, *Late in a Slow Time*
Suzanne Hancock, *Another Name for Bridge*
Jason Heroux, *Emergency Hallelujah*
Jason Heroux, *Memoirs of an Alias*
Jason Heroux, *Natural Capital*
John B. Lee, *In the Terrible Weather of Guns*
Jeanette Lynes, *The Aging Cheerleader's Alphabet*
David W. McFadden, *Be Calm, Honey*
David W. McFadden, *What's the Score?*
Leigh Nash, *Goodbye, Ukulele*
Lillian Necakov, *The Bone Broker*
Lillian Necakov, *Hooligans*
Peter Norman, *At the Gates of the Theme Park*
Natasha Nuhanovic, *Stray Dog Embassy*
Catherine Owen & Joe Rosenblatt, with Karen Moe, *Dog*
Corrado Paina, *The Alphabet of the Traveler*
Corrado Paina, *The Dowry of Education*
Corrado Paina, *Hoarse Legend*
Corrado Paina, *Souls in Plain Clothes*
Matt Santateresa, *A Beggar's Loom*
Matt Santateresa, *Icarus Redux*
Ann Shin, *The Last Thing Standing*
Jim Smith, *Back Off, Assassin! New and Selected Poems*
Jim Smith, *Happy Birthday, Nicanor Parra*
Robert Earl Stewart, *Campfire Radio Rhapsody*
Robert Earl Stewart, *Something Burned on the Southern Border*
Carey Toane, *The Crystal Palace*
Priscila Uppal, *Winter Sport: Poems*
Steve Venright, *Floors of Enduring Beauty*
Brian Wickers, *Stations of the Lost*

Fiction

Marianne Apostolides, *The Lucky Child*
Sarah Dearing, *The Art of Sufficient Conclusions*
Denis De Klerck, ed., *Particle & Wave: A Mansfield Omnibus of Electro-Magnetic Fiction*
Marko Sijan, *Mongrel*
Tom Walmsley, *Dog Eat Rat*

Non-Fiction

George Bowering, *How I Wrote Certain of My Books*
Denis De Klerck & Corrado Paina, eds., *College Street–Little Italy: Toronto's Renaissance Strip*
Pier Giorgio Di Cicco, *Municipal Mind: Manifestos for the Creative City*
Amy Lavender Harris, *Imagining Toronto*

To order Mansfield Press titles online, please visit mansfieldpress.net